Festive Tales for a Winter's Night

Leo .W.Forest

Published by Leo Forest, 2024.

This is a work of fiction. Similarities to real people, places, or events are entirely coincidental.

FESTIVE TALES FOR A WINTER'S NIGHT

First edition. October 13, 2024.

ISBN: 979-8227584359

Written by Leo .W.Forest.

The Snow Queen's Gift

IN THE VILLAGE OF FROSTHAVEN, the wind never ceased to howl, and the snow never stopped falling. The people of the village knew nothing but ice-capped roofs, frozen rivers, and a sky that was perpetually gray. Crops could not grow, and the sun seemed like a distant memory. No one could remember a time when warmth graced their land, for the curse of eternal winter had hung over Frosthaven for generations.

In the heart of the village lived a young girl named Elara. She was unlike most in Frosthaven, not because she was untouched by the cold, but because her spirit burned brighter than any fire. At fifteen, Elara was small but strong, with eyes the color of the winter sky—clear and determined. She lived with her grandmother in a modest cottage, its walls worn and its hearth rarely ablaze with anything more than a flicker of heat. Yet even in the biting cold, Elara's heart remained hopeful.

Each day, Elara watched the villagers struggle—elderly men and women hunched over, their limbs stiff from frost, and children with faces pale and gaunt, their laughter swallowed by the wind. But the worst was seeing her grandmother, once full of life, now weakened by the cold that seemed to seep into her bones. The village healer had little to offer but blankets and small fires, which did nothing against the curse.

Elara could not stand by any longer. Her village was dying, slowly and cruelly, trapped in a winter that had no end. Many had given up, accepting the frozen fate as inevitable. But not Elara. There had to be a way to break the curse, a way to bring warmth and light back to Frosthaven. She had heard the old stories, whispered by the elders, of the Snow Queen who lived far beyond the Northern Mountains, in a palace of ice. It was said that the Snow Queen held the power of winter in her hands, and that only by facing her could the curse be lifted.

Few dared to speak of the Snow Queen now—her name was associated with fear and mystery, and the treacherous journey to her palace had claimed the lives of those brave or desperate enough to try. But Elara had made up her mind. She would not let fear or the bitter cold stop her. She had to save her people, her grandmother, and her home.

One cold, starless night, Elara knelt beside her grandmother's bed. The old woman's breath was shallow, her hands cold despite the blankets. Elara grasped them, her heart heavy with love and determination.

"I'm going to the Snow Queen," Elara whispered, her voice steady despite the enormity of the task ahead. "I'll find her, and I'll end this curse."

Her grandmother's eyes fluttered open, filled with worry. "No one has ever returned, Elara," she said, her voice hoarse. "The Snow Queen... she is not like us. She has no heart to bargain with."

Elara squeezed her grandmother's hands tighter. "Then I won't bargain. I'll find a way to defeat her. I promise I'll return, and when I do, there will be warmth again."

Her grandmother did not argue. She knew the strength of Elara's will. Instead, she nodded weakly, her lips parting in a soft prayer to the old gods for her granddaughter's safe return.

Elara spent the next few days preparing for her journey. She gathered supplies—what little food she could find, a thick woolen cloak, and a small knife sheathed at her belt. She knew the path ahead would be perilous, but her heart was set. The villagers whispered as she passed, their voices low with both admiration and fear. Some tried to dissuade her, others simply watched with silent hope.

As Elara stood at the edge of the village, the wind biting at her face, she cast one last look over Frosthaven. The snow swirled like a ghostly mist around the darkened cottages, and for a moment, doubt crept into her mind. But then she remembered the faces of the people she loved—their suffering, their resilience—and the doubt vanished. She would do this for them, no matter the cost.

Pulling her cloak tighter around her shoulders, Elara turned her back on the village and set off toward the Northern Mountains, her heart burning with the promise of hope.

Elara had been walking for hours. The snow crunched beneath her boots, and the wind stung her face, but she pressed on, her eyes fixed on the distant silhouette of the Northern Mountains. Each step grew heavier as the biting cold seeped deeper into her bones. The world around her was a desolate expanse of white, and for the first time, she began to understand why so many had failed this journey.

Just as doubt began to creep into her heart, she heard it—a soft, rhythmic sound, like bells tinkling in the distance. At first, Elara thought it was a trick of the wind, but as the sound grew closer, she turned and gasped.

Emerging from the swirling snow was a magnificent reindeer, its coat shimmering as if dusted with frost. Its antlers glistened like crystal, catching the faint moonlight, and around its neck hung a wreath of silver bells that jingled with each step. Its eyes, deep and wise, met Elara's, and in that moment, she knew this creature was no ordinary reindeer.

The reindeer paused a few feet from her, its breath misting in the cold air. Elara stood frozen, both in awe and confusion. She had heard of magical creatures in the old stories, but never had she imagined one would appear before her.

"Who are you?" Elara whispered, her voice barely audible over the wind.

The reindeer lowered its head in a graceful bow, as if understanding her question. Then, in a voice that seemed to echo in her mind rather than through the air, it spoke.

"I am Auron, guardian of the Northern Path," the reindeer said, its voice calm and soothing. "I have been sent to guide you, Elara of Frosthaven."

Elara blinked in astonishment. "Sent? By whom?"

"The Snow Queen knows you are coming," Auron replied, his eyes shimmering with a knowing light. "She is expecting you."

A chill ran down Elara's spine, though it wasn't from the cold. She had hoped to reach the Snow Queen unnoticed, to find some way to convince or trick her into lifting the curse. But now, it seemed the Queen was already aware of her quest.

"Why would she send you to help me?" Elara asked, her voice tinged with suspicion. "If she knows I'm coming, doesn't that mean she's ready to stop me?"

Auron shook his head gently, the bells around his neck jingling softly. "The Queen is not as you imagine, young one. She will not harm you, but neither will she make this easy. The path is fraught with trials, and only the worthy may reach her palace. I am here to ensure you do not lose your way."

Elara's heart raced. She had expected the journey to be dangerous, but now it seemed the Snow Queen had more in store for her than she could have anticipated. Still, there was no turning back.

"I'll face whatever trials she gives me," Elara said, her voice resolute. "I have to save my village."

Auron nodded, his eyes reflecting her determination. “Then climb onto my back, and I will take you to her palace. Time is short, and the journey is long.”

Without hesitation, Elara stepped forward and grasped the reindeer’s thick, soft fur. With a graceful leap, she mounted Auron, her hands clutching his shimmering mane. The moment she was settled, Auron began to move, his powerful legs gliding effortlessly over the snow.

They traveled faster than Elara could have imagined. The world blurred around them, the endless white landscape rushing past in a whirl of wind and snow. Yet, on Auron’s back, Elara felt strangely warm, as though a protective barrier shielded her from the freezing cold.

Hours passed like minutes, and soon the jagged peaks of the Northern Mountains loomed ahead, their icy slopes gleaming in the moonlight. Elara’s heart quickened—she was getting closer.

As they reached the base of the mountains, Auron slowed, then stopped. He turned his head to look back at Elara, his eyes filled with quiet encouragement.

“This is as far as I can take you,” Auron said softly. “Beyond this point, the trials begin. You must face them alone.”

Elara slid off his back, her feet sinking into the snow. She looked up at the towering mountains ahead, a mix of fear and determination surging within her.

“Thank you, Auron,” she said, her voice firm despite the fluttering in her chest. “I won’t fail.”

The reindeer bowed once more. “May your heart guide you true, Elara of Frosthaven. Remember, the Snow Queen’s riddles are more than they seem.”

With that, Auron turned and vanished into the snowstorm, leaving Elara standing alone at the foot of the icy mountains. The palace of the Snow Queen awaited her, its entrance hidden somewhere among the frozen peaks.

Taking a deep breath, Elara steeled herself for what lay ahead. The real journey had just begun.

ELARA CLIMBED THE ICY slopes of the Northern Mountains, her breath heavy in the frozen air. Each step was harder than the last, her hands and feet numbed by the relentless cold. Yet, despite the exhaustion, she pressed on, driven by the thought of her village—her grandmother—and the people depending on her. After what felt like hours, she reached the top of a ridge, and there it stood—the Snow Queen's palace.

It was a towering fortress of ice, its walls gleaming like glass, catching the pale light of the winter sun. The palace looked both beautiful and forbidding, its sharp spires reaching into the sky as if piercing the heavens. Elara's heart pounded in her chest as she approached the massive doors, etched with intricate frost patterns. With trembling hands, she pushed them open.

Inside, the air was unnaturally still, and the vast hall before her shimmered in shades of blue and white. At the far end, seated on a throne carved from pure ice, was the Snow Queen. She was as radiant as the legends said—her gown made of glittering frost, her hair cascading like snow, and her eyes cold and piercing.

"I have been expecting you, Elara of Frosthaven," the Snow Queen's voice echoed through the hall, soft but filled with power.

Elara swallowed her fear and stepped forward. "I've come to end the curse," she said, her voice steady. "My village can't survive any longer under this eternal winter."

The Snow Queen's lips curved into a faint smile. "Brave words," she said, rising from her throne. "But words alone cannot break the curse. If you wish to save your people, you must prove yourself worthy. I will give you three riddles. Solve them, and the curse will be lifted. Fail, and you will remain here in my palace—forever frozen in time."

Elara's stomach tightened, but she nodded, her resolve unwavering. "I accept."

The Snow Queen waved her hand, and before Elara, three pillars of ice rose from the ground, each one glowing with a faint, magical light.

"Here is your first riddle," the Snow Queen said, her voice as cold as the air around them. "I am not alive, but I grow. I don't have lungs, but I need air. What am I?"

Elara frowned, her mind racing. She closed her eyes, trying to picture the riddle. Something that isn't alive but grows? No lungs, but it needs air? And then it came to her, like a spark in the darkness.

"A fire," she said confidently. "The answer is fire."

The Snow Queen's eyes gleamed with approval, and one of the pillars of ice shattered into a burst of snowflakes. "Correct. But the next will not be so easy."

She stepped closer, her presence filling the room with an icy chill. "Here is your second riddle: The more you take, the more you leave behind. What am I?"

Elara furrowed her brow. She had heard this riddle before, but in her exhaustion and the pressure of the moment, the answer seemed to slip from her grasp. She took a deep breath, calming her racing thoughts. The more you take... the more you leave behind.

Footsteps. The answer was footsteps.

"Footsteps," she said aloud, feeling her confidence return.

The second pillar of ice shattered, and the Snow Queen nodded once more, though her expression remained unreadable.

"You are clever," she admitted, her voice softer now. "But there is one final riddle. Answer this, and your people will be free." The Snow Queen's eyes bore into Elara's, as if measuring her very soul.

The final pillar of ice began to glow brightly, casting an eerie light around the hall. The Snow Queen's voice was low, almost a whisper. "I am something that cannot be seen, cannot be touched, yet it is stronger than iron, more valuable than gold. What am I?"

Elara froze. This riddle was different—deeper, more elusive. She paced the cold floor, her mind working furiously. Something invisible but stronger than iron, more valuable than gold? She thought of all the things she had encountered on her journey, but nothing fit.

Frustration clawed at her. What could it be?

And then, as she stood in the silence of the icy hall, she remembered something her grandmother had once told her: The strongest things in this world are those that cannot be held in your hands, but only in your heart.

Elara's breath caught. The answer wasn't a thing. It was a feeling, a force that had driven her to make this journey, that had kept her moving even when the cold was unbearable.

"Love," she said, her voice quiet but certain. "The answer is love."

For a moment, there was only silence. Then, with a deafening crack, the final pillar shattered, sending a flurry of ice and snow through the hall. The Snow Queen stood still, her eyes softening as if the ice that encased her heart had melted, even if just for a moment.

"You are right," the Snow Queen said, her voice almost gentle. "Love is indeed stronger than any curse."

With a wave of her hand, the ice palace began to shimmer and dissolve, the cold air warming slightly. The eternal winter that had gripped Frosthaven for so long was beginning to fade.

"You have proven yourself, Elara," the Snow Queen said, her form becoming faint like a mist. "Go home, and know that your people are free."

Before Elara could respond, the Snow Queen and her palace vanished, leaving her standing alone on the now thawing mountainside.

Elara's journey was over. She had solved the riddles, not with strength or cunning alone, but with heart. And now, the curse was lifted.

As the Snow Queen's palace dissolved around her, Elara felt an overwhelming sense of peace, but her heart still raced with the weight of the final riddle's truth. The answer had not been fire or footsteps, but something deeper—love. And it wasn't just a clever solution to a puzzle. Love had been the force guiding her throughout this journey, driving her to risk everything for her village.

But there was something more—something the Snow Queen hadn't revealed.

As the last remnants of ice faded, a warm breeze began to blow through the mountains. The eternal winter was finally breaking. The snow that had piled high in the village for years now melted, and for the first time in Elara's life, she could feel the touch of warmth in the air.

Yet, in the pit of her stomach, she knew her journey wasn't quite finished. The Snow Queen had lifted the curse, but there was a final choice to be made. Standing there in the thawing wilderness, Elara heard the Snow Queen's voice in her mind, soft but unmistakable.

"True love is not about what it can give you, but what you are willing to sacrifice. You have proven yourself wise, Elara, but now you must prove that you are selfless. To fully break the curse, you must leave behind what you cherish most."

Elara froze, the weight of the words sinking in. What she cherished most? It didn't take her long to understand. Her heart clenched as her thoughts immediately turned to her grandmother, her village, and the life she had fought so hard to return to.

Her pulse quickened, and doubt clouded her mind. She had done everything she could to save Frosthaven. She had endured the harshest cold, risked her life solving the Snow Queen's riddles, and now—she was being asked to give up the one thing she had wanted more than anything: to return home.

Tears stung her eyes as she considered her choices. She could refuse, but then the curse would never truly lift. The Snow Queen's trials weren't just about testing her cleverness. They were about seeing if she could embrace something bigger than herself.

Elara stood still, breathing deeply, letting the reality of her decision settle. If it meant Frosthaven would live, if it meant her grandmother could grow old without suffering, and the children could run through fields no longer blanketed in endless snow—then her choice was already made.

She wiped her tears away and stood tall, lifting her face to the clearing sky. "I understand," she whispered. "If my village is to be free, I will not return."

In that moment, the air shimmered around her, and she felt an immense warmth spread through her body. The last of the cold slipped away, and the Snow Queen's voice echoed one final time in her mind.

"You have chosen well. The true power of love lies not in what it grants, but in what it asks of us. Your selflessness has broken the curse."

The warmth intensified, but it was not an uncomfortable heat. It felt like the embrace of something greater than herself—like the love she had always felt for her people, magnified a thousandfold. She closed her eyes, and when she opened them again, she found herself standing in the center of her village.

The eternal winter had vanished. The snow had melted, and the fields were green, with flowers blooming as if spring had arrived overnight. Elara's village was alive again, its people standing in awe at the sudden transformation. Children ran through the streets, their laughter echoing through the air, and Elara's heart swelled with joy.

But as she looked around, she realized something strange. Though her village was thriving, she stood apart—unseen by the others. Her grandmother was there, smiling and happy, her frail hands no longer shaking with the cold. Her friends and neighbors embraced one another in joy, but none of them could see her.

Elara understood. The Snow Queen had kept her word. Her sacrifice had lifted the curse, but in doing so, she had left behind her place among them. She had given them their lives back, even if it meant stepping into the shadows.

And so, Elara stood silently at the edge of her village, watching the people she loved so dearly live in peace. She had saved them—not with cleverness or strength, but with love and selflessness.

Elara watched from the edge of her village as the warm sun kissed the earth, melting away the last traces of winter. Flowers bloomed, birds chirped, and the people of Frosthaven danced in the streets, rejoicing in the return of the seasons they had long forgotten. Elara's heart was full, knowing her sacrifice had saved them, even if she had been unseen and unrecognized in the process.

But just as she was about to turn away, ready to accept her new reality, a soft, familiar voice called out.

"Elara..."

The voice was gentle, and the air around her shimmered. Out of the soft light stepped the Snow Queen, but this time, she wasn't cloaked in ice and cold. Her appearance was softer, her frosty gown now a delicate silver, glowing with a warm light. The Queen's expression wasn't cold or distant, but kind.

"You have proven yourself in ways I did not expect," the Snow Queen said, her voice filled with quiet admiration. "Your love and sacrifice have freed your people, but you are not meant to remain unseen."

Elara blinked in surprise, her breath catching in her throat.

"You gave up everything for them," the Snow Queen continued. "And for that, I offer you something greater than a simple reward."

With a wave of her hand, the Snow Queen's magic filled the air. Elara felt a warmth rush through her body, and suddenly, the villagers' eyes turned toward her. Her grandmother, who had been standing in the village square, gasped in recognition.

"Elara!" her grandmother cried, her voice breaking with emotion.

Before Elara could react, her grandmother rushed toward her, her eyes shining with tears of joy. The villagers, too, began to gather around, murmuring her name, their faces lit with gratitude. Her friends, her neighbors, the children—everyone she had fought so hard to save—now saw her for the hero she was.

"You've saved us, Elara," her grandmother said, pulling her into a tight embrace. "You're our hero."

Elara smiled through her own tears, overwhelmed by the love and warmth surrounding her. She hadn't expected to return as a hero. She hadn't expected to return at all. But now, standing among her people, the weight of her journey lifted. She had done what she set out to do—she had saved them.

The Snow Queen watched from the edge of the village, her expression soft but unreadable. As the villagers continued to celebrate Elara's return, the Queen's form began to fade, but before she disappeared entirely, her voice whispered one final message to Elara.

"Remember, true power lies in love and selflessness. You've shown the strength of your heart. Your people are free because of you."

And with that, the Snow Queen vanished, leaving only the warmth of her magic behind.

Elara looked up at the bright, clear sky, feeling the sun on her face for the first time in years. Her village was alive again, her people safe, and though she had sacrificed much, she had gained something far greater: the love of her people and the knowledge that she had done something truly extraordinary.

As the village continued to celebrate, Elara stood at the heart of it all, embraced by those she had fought for. And though the snow had melted and the cold was gone, the lessons she had learned on her journey would stay with her forever.

She was home. And she was a hero.

Twelve Days of Christmas Mysteries

DETECTIVE MAXIMUS "MAX" Finch wasn't your typical village detective. At first glance, he seemed rather unremarkable—a short man in his late forties with a perpetually rumpled tweed jacket, an ever-growing collection of patterned scarves, and a penchant for cinnamon tea. What truly set Max apart, however, was his remarkable ability to solve even the strangest of mysteries with a combination of wit, charm, and an eccentric, yet methodical, approach to crime-solving.

The village of Hollybrook, where Max resided and practiced his detective work, was just as whimsical as he was. Nestled in the rolling English countryside, the village was known for its cobblestone streets, ivy-covered cottages, and an annual Christmas festival that rivaled any in the county. Every December, the whole village seemed to come alive with twinkling lights, decorated shop windows, and the scent of mulled wine and freshly baked gingerbread wafting through the crisp air.

It was the kind of place where everyone knew everyone, and gossip traveled faster than Santa's sleigh on Christmas Eve. Despite its quaint charm, Hollybrook had a reputation for attracting peculiar happenings, especially during the holiday season. And this year, with Christmas only days away, something strange was already afoot.

Max strolled through the village square, savoring the festive atmosphere. The towering Christmas tree at the center was adorned with shimmering baubles and a star that glittered in the winter sun. Children played near a snow-covered fountain, their laughter filling the air as they chased each other with snowballs. Villagers greeted Max warmly as he passed by, tipping their hats or offering a cheerful "Happy Christmas, Detective!"

Hollybrook had a way of wrapping itself in warmth during the coldest months, but the detective's mind never fully rested, not even in the most peaceful of settings. He observed everything—the irregular footprints in the snow, the faint smell of cinnamon mixed with something else in the air, and the curious way old Mrs. Haversham had been staring at the bakery window for far too long.

Max's usual day involved keeping an eye on the small village, though crime was rare. A lost cat, a misplaced scarf, or the occasional case of stolen biscuits from the bakery. All in a day's work. But this December felt different. There was an unusual hum in the village—a quiet anticipation that Max couldn't quite place. It was as though the very air was holding its breath, waiting for something to happen.

As he reached the edge of the square, he was greeted by the bustling scene at Mistletoe & Magic, Hollybrook's finest (and only) gift shop, run by the ever-enthusiastic Pippa Goodwin. Max tipped his hat as Pippa waved from the window, her hands busily wrapping a customer's purchase in red and green paper.

"Detective Finch!" Pippa called, her voice bright. "Do stop by later! I've got the finest mince pies ready for you!"

Max smiled and raised a hand in acknowledgement but continued on his walk. He had a feeling he would need his wits about him in the coming days, and sugar wasn't going to help.

The sky above was beginning to darken, but the village twinkled with light. Max paused by the old church, his sharp eyes catching something unusual on the notice board. Among the usual advertisements for the Christmas Eve choir and the yuletide bake sale was a freshly pinned notice: Missing: Partridge and Pear Tree. Last seen at Greenbriar Manor. Any information, please contact.

Max raised an eyebrow. A missing partridge and pear tree? On the first day of Christmas, no less. The detective's curiosity piqued. This was going to be no ordinary holiday season in Hollybrook.

“Looks like the festivities just got interesting,” Max murmured to himself, pulling his scarf tighter against the chill. Something was brewing in the village, and as always, he was ready to unravel the mystery—one missing item at a time.

Max Finch had barely made it home, settled into his armchair, and poured himself a steaming cup of cinnamon tea when the phone rang. He sighed, setting the cup down. "Always right before the tea," he muttered, picking up the receiver.

"Detective Finch? It's Mrs. Haversham," came the breathless voice on the other end. "There's been a theft at Greenbriar Manor. You must come quickly—this is very peculiar!"

Max straightened. Greenbriar Manor was the grandest house in Hollybrook, home to the eccentric Lady Winifred Beauregard. If anything strange was going to happen, it was likely to be there. "What exactly has gone missing, Mrs. Haversham?"

"A partridge, Detective! And a pear tree! The whole thing vanished from the garden!"

Max blinked. A partridge and a pear tree? This was no ordinary theft. "I'll be there in ten minutes," he said, grabbing his coat and scarf before hanging up.

The crisp winter air greeted Max as he stepped outside. The walk to Greenbriar Manor was short, and soon enough, he was at the towering gates of the estate. The manor itself loomed in the distance, festively adorned with wreaths and glowing lights. Mrs. Haversham, Lady Winifred's housekeeper, was waiting at the entrance, wringing her hands.

"Come quickly, Detective," she urged. "It's most unusual."

Max followed her through the frosted garden, his sharp eyes scanning the surroundings. The ground was untouched except for a few faint footprints leading toward a large, empty patch near the fountain—where, he presumed, the pear tree had once stood.

"Tell me what happened," Max said, crouching down to examine the prints.

Mrs. Haversham adjusted her woolen shawl. "It was this morning. I came out to tend to the garden, and the pear tree—along with that lovely partridge Lady Winifred had imported—was gone! Not a trace left behind. I thought it might be some prank, but it's such an odd thing to steal, don't you think?"

Max glanced up at her. "Did anyone visit the manor recently? Anyone acting strangely?"

Mrs. Haversham shook her head. "Not a soul. Lady Winifred is away visiting her sister, and the estate has been quiet. Only me, the gardener, and the cook around."

Max nodded, standing up. "Show me where the pear tree was."

Mrs. Haversham led him to the now-empty patch of earth. It was clear that something had been hastily removed—a slight disturbance in the soil and broken branches indicated the tree had been uprooted quickly.

Max knelt to inspect the area more closely. Among the muddled prints, he spotted a fresh clue: a single feather—small, gray, and unmistakably belonging to a partridge. He plucked it from the ground, holding it up for Mrs. Haversham to see.

"A feather?" she asked, her brow furrowed.

"Indeed," Max said, slipping it into his pocket. "It seems our thief wasn't very careful."

He straightened and looked around once more, piecing together the scenario. The theft wasn't random—someone had deliberately taken both the bird and the tree. And given the timing, this was no coincidence.

"The first day of Christmas," Max murmured thoughtfully. "A partridge in a pear tree."

Mrs. Haversham blinked. "What was that, Detective?"

Max smiled slightly. "I think someone's decided to make this Christmas a bit of a puzzle, Mrs. Haversham. And I suspect we're only just beginning."

With a nod of thanks, Max turned and headed back toward the village, already forming a plan. If this thief was following the famous carol, then tomorrow promised to bring even more peculiarities. He had a feeling the next eleven days would keep him on his toes.

And Max Finch, never one to shy away from a mystery, was more than ready for the challenge.

Over the next few days, Hollybrook's festive spirit became tinged with curiosity and confusion. True to Max's suspicion, each morning brought another baffling theft, matching the lyrics of the "12 Days of Christmas."

On the second day, two turtle doves went missing from Mrs. Pippa Goodwin's aviary. "I just woke up, and the cage door was wide open!" she exclaimed to Max. "No sign of a break-in, no nothing!" Max found a feather near the cage, just like at Greenbriar Manor.

The third day brought three missing French hens from Mr. O'Malley's farm. Max interviewed him while O'Malley stood fuming, arms crossed. "I've raised those hens from eggs, Detective! Who in their right mind steals chickens?"

Each theft followed the carol like clockwork. Four calling birds vanished from the pet shop. Five golden rings disappeared from the village jeweler's window display, leaving the owner, Mrs. Fairweather, in a state of panic. Max began to wonder how far this Christmas caper would go.

By day six, Max had a growing list of suspects. He kept a notebook with details of everyone who had connections to the stolen items. The gardener at Greenbriar Manor seemed overly interested in the goings-on at the estate, and Mr. O'Malley's neighbor had been eyeing those hens for months. Pippa Goodwin's shop had plenty of visitors, any of whom could have tampered with the birdcages.

On the seventh day, seven swans went missing from the village pond. The swans were the pride of Hollybrook's winter display, and their disappearance caused an uproar. "They're not easy to hide, are they?" Max muttered, noting the lack of tracks around the pond. "Someone knows what they're doing."

By now, word of the strange thefts had spread, and villagers were eager to help, though most of their theories were more colorful than useful. Some suspected a group of mischievous kids, others thought it was an elaborate prank orchestrated by a bored local. But Max wasn't convinced. This felt too deliberate.

On the eighth day, eight milkmaids were suddenly without their cows, as the animals had been led out of their barns overnight. As Max interviewed the farmers, he noticed a pattern: in each case, the thief had been careful not to leave too many clues behind—except for a few feathers, hoof prints, and faint traces of hay.

By day nine, the village was in a frenzy. Nine ladies in the Hollybrook dance troupe arrived at their morning rehearsal to find their dancing shoes had vanished. "What kind of thief steals shoes?" one of them huffed to Max, pointing at the empty spot in the studio.

Max spent hours following leads, listening to rumors, and combing through clues. His notebook was filled with interviews, sketches of footprints, and observations. He had narrowed his suspects down to a few key individuals, but he was still missing the crucial connection that tied them all together.

On the tenth day, ten lords—actually, ten gentlemen from the village's fencing club—reported that their swords had disappeared. This theft left Max more puzzled than ever. Stealing animals or jewelry was one thing, but what could anyone possibly want with fencing swords?

The eleventh day saw the disappearance of eleven pipes from the local pub, The Merry Piper. Old man Higgins, the owner, was furious. "Those pipes were antique! Worth a fortune!"

By now, Max was almost certain he knew who the culprit was. The clues had started forming a clearer picture. It wasn't just random theft—it was someone deeply involved in the village's Christmas traditions. The thief was smart, careful, and playing a game, likely for reasons beyond material gain.

On the twelfth day, as the village gathered for the Christmas Eve festival, Max prepared himself. The last item—twelve drums from the village band—had vanished that morning. Max was sure the thief would be in the crowd tonight, watching their handiwork unfold.

As the lights twinkled across the village square, Max Finch was ready to confront the mastermind behind the Twelve Days of Christmas mystery. The festive night wasn't over yet, and the solution was just within reach.

The village square buzzed with excitement. Hollybrook's Christmas Eve festival was in full swing—children laughing, carolers singing, and a warm glow from the lights hanging between the shops. But Max Finch wasn't in the mood for merriment. He stood near the fountain, eyes scanning the crowd. Tonight, he'd solve the Twelve Days of Christmas mystery.

As the mayor took the stage to start the night's performances, Max noticed a figure lingering near the back of the square. It was Mrs. Haversham, Lady Winifred's housekeeper. She was acting strangely—hovering near the tents, trying not to be noticed. Max's eyes narrowed. She had been at the center of this from the start.

Max approached her quietly, stepping out from the shadows. "Mrs. Haversham," he said, catching her off guard. "You've been rather busy these last twelve days, haven't you?"

Her face turned pale, then flushed red. "I—I don't know what you mean, Detective," she stammered.

"Oh, but I think you do," Max said gently. "The partridge, the hens, the swans, even the drums. They all vanished under your watch. And now, here you are—looking a bit guilty."

Mrs. Haversham sighed heavily, her shoulders slumping. "Alright, alright, you've caught me." She looked embarrassed but not defensive. "But it's not what you think."

Max folded his arms, waiting.

"I didn't steal those things for myself," she explained. "Lady Winifred has been so lonely lately, and I thought—well, I thought if I recreated the '12 Days of Christmas,' it would cheer her up when she returned. She always loved that song, you see, and I wanted to make it real for her. I didn't mean to cause such a fuss."

Max blinked. "So, you stole everything to create the twelve days of Christmas for Lady Winifred?"

Mrs. Haversham nodded sheepishly. "Yes, but I had planned to return everything after Christmas. I've kept everything safe in the manor. The animals, the rings, even the drums—they're all there, waiting for her."

Max couldn't help but chuckle. "Well, you certainly had the village in a frenzy, Mrs. Haversham. But your heart was in the right place."

Her eyes softened. "I'm sorry, Detective. I didn't think it would spiral out of control like this."

Max smiled warmly. "Don't worry. I'll explain things to the mayor. But next time, maybe ask before borrowing half the village's possessions."

With a nod of understanding, Mrs. Haversham let out a sigh of relief. "Thank you, Detective Finch."

Max tipped his hat. "Merry Christmas, Mrs. Haversham. And let's make sure Lady Winifred enjoys the best surprise of her life."

As the Christmas lights twinkled above, Max walked back toward the square, his heart lightened. The mystery had been solved, and in the end, it wasn't about theft—it was about spreading a little unexpected joy.

By Christmas morning, the village of Hollybrook had heard the full story. Instead of being outraged, the villagers were touched by Mrs. Haversham's gesture. After all, Christmas was about kindness, generosity, and a little bit of whimsy.

Max helped organize the return of all the stolen items. The partridge was back in its pear tree at Greenbriar Manor, the swans were safely returned to the pond, and even the fencing club's swords had been neatly placed back in their racks. Mrs. Fairweather was particularly relieved to see her five golden rings again.

The village, far from being upset, found themselves smiling at the whole affair. The absurdity of the situation had brought everyone together, reminding them that the holiday spirit wasn't in material things but in the joy they shared with one another.

That evening, the Christmas Eve festival resumed with even more energy. The villagers gathered in the square for a grand feast, laughter filling the air as they recalled the 12 days of confusion. Mrs. Haversham stood beside Lady Winifred, who was delighted by the whole story.

Max, watching from a distance, took in the scene with satisfaction. For once, a case had ended with more cheer than it began.

As the clock struck midnight and the first flakes of snow began to fall, the villagers raised their glasses in a toast. "To Hollybrook!" the mayor cheered. "And to the true meaning of Christmas!"

Max couldn't help but smile. Sometimes, even a detective needs a reminder that the best mysteries aren't solved with logic alone—they're solved with heart.

Letters to the Spirit of Christmas

Margaret sat by the window, watching the soft December snow blanket the garden outside. Her small home, nestled at the end of a quiet street, was filled with the echoes of years gone by. Faded photographs lined the mantel, each frame capturing a moment of laughter, of birthdays, of Christmases spent with family. The scent of pine from the tree in the corner mingled with the faint aroma of peppermint tea, creating an air of quiet warmth.

Every year, this was her ritual: sitting down at her kitchen table, pen in hand, to write her Christmas letter. It had become more than a tradition. It was a way of connecting with her children and grandchildren, scattered across different cities, living lives too busy to visit often. They had come to expect these letters—simple, handwritten reflections of the year passed, tied up with wishes for the year to come.

But this year was different.

Margaret glanced at the stack of unopened cards from friends and neighbors, feeling the weight of time. She was alone now, her husband gone for nearly a decade, her days quiet save for the ticking of the clock and the hum of the heater. The solitude didn't bother her as much as it once had; it had become familiar, even comforting in its own way. Still, the letters had become a lifeline—a tangible way to feel close to the family she loved so dearly.

She smoothed a fresh sheet of paper before her, the pen poised in her frail hand. As always, she would write about the year's happenings: births, milestones, small victories. But there was something more this time, something pressing at the edges of her heart. Margaret knew, deep down, that this would be her final Christmas letter. A decision she had made with quiet certainty.

And with that thought, her mind drifted to the secret she had kept for so long. Would this be the year she finally shared it?

Margaret pressed the tip of her pen to the paper, her hand trembling slightly. She began with the usual greetings, carefully crafting words of warmth and love for each of her children and grandchildren. The act of writing steadied her, the familiar rhythm of her thoughts flowing into each sentence. She spoke of the winter's chill, of her neighbor's new puppy, and how she had taken up knitting again, just small things to share. But as the ink spread across the page, she felt the weight of the unspoken pull at her.

Her eyes wandered to the small box tucked on the bookshelf. It had been there for decades, undisturbed, yet its contents had never left her mind. Inside was a bundle of letters—ones she had written, and one she had never sent. The one that changed her life.

Margaret paused, her breath catching. She had never told anyone about that summer. It was the summer before she married her husband, the one everyone had known about, the man she had built her life with. But there had been someone else, a fleeting, passionate love she had shared with a man whose name she had never spoken aloud again. Not even to herself.

His name was James.

The memories came back in sharp clarity, as if they had been waiting all these years, just beneath the surface. She had been young, reckless with her heart, and filled with dreams of adventure. James had appeared like a spark in her life—a handsome, kind-hearted man who made her feel alive in a way she hadn't known was possible. They had met at a summer fair, under the bright lights of a Ferris wheel. She could still hear the laughter in the air, the sound of the carousel music, and the way his smile had made her heart race.

But it was brief, only a few months before circumstances pulled them apart. Her family had expected her to marry someone else, someone steady and reliable. And so, Margaret had made a choice—a painful, necessary choice to walk away from James and into the life she thought was meant for her.

She had never spoken of him, never mentioned that brief, intense love that had burned so brightly before being extinguished. The letter she had written to him, explaining her decision, remained unsent in that box. She had buried it deep, alongside the part of her heart that still ached for what could have been.

Margaret blinked back tears as she stared at the empty space on the page. She had never told her children, her grandchildren—no one knew of the sacrifice she had made, the secret she had carried for a lifetime.

Now, after so many years, she wondered: Should they know? Would it change how they saw her? Would it matter?

Her pen hovered over the paper, the decision looming before her. She had started this letter with the intention of ending a chapter. But perhaps it was time to open another.

Margaret set the pen down and rubbed her temples, feeling the weight of her past press heavily on her. The room, once filled with warmth from the fire, now felt smaller, as if the walls were closing in. The memories of James, and of the life she had chosen not to pursue, were swirling around her like a gust of winter wind that wouldn't settle.

She stood and walked to the bookshelf, her hand hesitating before reaching for the small, worn box. Her fingers grazed the dusty lid, and she lifted it slowly, as if handling something fragile. Inside, beneath layers of yellowed letters, was the one she had written to James all those years ago, tucked neatly at the bottom, untouched since the day she had sealed it. It was the letter she had poured her heart into, the one explaining why she couldn't be with him, even though she had wanted to more than anything.

For years, she had convinced herself that this secret belonged to another life, a chapter closed so long ago that it didn't belong to the woman her family knew now. Her children and grandchildren saw her as the matriarch, the one who had held them all together, through every Christmas, every hardship, and every celebration. To them, she had always been strong, steady, and unfaltering.

But the truth was more complicated. The truth was that Margaret had been in love with two men in her lifetime, and the one she had lost had never fully left her. Her marriage to her husband, David, had been filled with love and devotion, but deep down, a part of her had always wondered what her life would have been like if she had followed her heart that summer. She had made the choice to build a family, to live the life that was expected of her, and she had no regrets. But the ache for what could have been lingered in her heart, a quiet reminder of the path not taken.

As she stared at the letter, memories began to flood back—James's laugh, the way he'd looked at her under the stars, the promises they had whispered to each other in the moonlight. They had planned to run away together, to build a life of adventure, one without the expectations that weighed so heavily on Margaret back then. But reality had crept in. Her father had become ill, and her family needed her. And there was David, waiting patiently, offering stability and love in a way James never could. Margaret had chosen what was best for everyone else, leaving her heart's desire behind.

Now, as she sat back down at her desk, the weight of that choice pressed down on her, harder than ever before. Her hand trembled as she picked up her pen once more, staring at the unfinished letter in front of her.

Should she tell them? Should she reveal this chapter of her life that no one knew existed?

The thought filled her with doubt. Her children had always seen her as wise, practical, someone who had made all the right decisions.

Would they understand? Would they feel betrayed to know she had hidden such a profound part of herself from them all these years? And what about her grandchildren, who looked up to her with such admiration? Would they see her differently if they knew the story of her lost love?

Margaret wrestled with these questions, her heart heavy with uncertainty. Part of her wanted to protect them from this truth, to keep the image they had of her intact. But another part of her—an older, quieter part—felt that maybe it was time to share her full self with them. She had always taught her children to be honest, to live with integrity. How could she keep this part of her life hidden any longer?

Her mind churned with conflicting thoughts. She imagined their reactions: confusion, surprise, maybe even anger. But then she thought of the deeper lessons they could learn from her story—that life is full of hard choices, that love is complicated, and that sometimes, sacrifices are made out of necessity, not weakness.

Margaret set the pen down again, staring out the window at the snow-covered trees. A lifetime of memories lay in front of her, scattered like snowflakes, each one unique and precious. She had always believed that her family deserved to know the truth, but now that the moment had come, she hesitated. Once she wrote these words, there would be no taking them back.

She sighed, closing her eyes, and let the memories wash over her again. The love she had shared with James, and the love she had found with David—they were both real, both important parts of who she was. But could she trust her family to understand that? Would they see the complexity of her choices, or would they feel hurt by the things she had never told them?

The thought of her family sitting together, reading this final letter at Christmas, filled her with both fear and hope. Perhaps they would be angry, or perhaps they would be grateful to know the full story of their mother and grandmother—a woman who had lived a life of love, loss, and choices that shaped them all.

She picked up the pen once more, her decision still unclear, but her heart knowing that the truth, once set free, would offer her peace—no matter the outcome.

Margaret sat in silence for a long time, her fingers lightly tracing the edge of the paper, the pen lying motionless beside her. The house was quiet, save for the occasional creak of the floorboards and the ticking of the old grandfather clock in the hallway. She could hear the faint hum of the wind outside, the snowstorm growing thicker. Her mind wrestled with the decision before her, the weight of it pressing heavily on her chest.

It was strange, she thought, how one moment could define so much of a person's life. For decades, she had carried this secret, safely tucked away in her heart. She had convinced herself it was for the best, that some truths were better left untold, buried beneath the life she had chosen to build. But now, nearing the end of her journey, Margaret felt the undeniable pull to share the full story of who she had been—of the sacrifices she had made, of the love she had lost.

She reached for her pen with trembling fingers, took a deep breath, and began to write.

"My dearest family," she wrote, her words deliberate, each stroke of the pen measured. "I have spent many Christmases writing letters to you, sharing stories of the past year, of the joys and challenges we've faced together. This year, however, I feel that I must share something more. Something I have kept to myself for far too long."

Her heart pounded as she continued, feeling the pull of memories, both sweet and bitter.

"Before I married your father, there was someone else. His name was James. We met when I was a young woman, full of dreams and hopes, at a time in my life when I thought the world was wide open to me. James and I shared a deep, passionate love, one that felt like a fire burning inside me. He was everything I thought I wanted—adventurous, free-spirited, and kind."

Margaret paused, the tip of her pen hovering over the page. She could see James as clearly as if he were standing before her—the way he used to look at her with such tenderness, the way his laughter had made her feel like the happiest girl in the world.

"We planned to run away together, to leave behind the expectations of our families and build a life of our own. For a brief moment, I believed that was possible. But life, as it often does, had other plans."

Her hand shook slightly as she wrote the next words, the memories flooding back with a vividness that startled her.

"That summer, my father became ill. Our family was struggling, and I was needed at home. James was ready to leave, but I couldn't walk away from my family. They needed me more than ever, and deep down, I knew that the life I had imagined with James wasn't meant to be. I had responsibilities, ones that I couldn't ignore, no matter how much my heart ached for him."

Margaret's breath hitched, her chest tightening as the emotions from that time surged forward. She had never forgotten the look on James's face when she told him she couldn't go with him—the hurt, the disappointment. He had pleaded with her to reconsider, to choose him. But Margaret had already made her choice, even if it had broken her heart.

"I made the decision to stay," she wrote, her words flowing more easily now. "I wrote James a letter, explaining that I couldn't follow him, that my duty to my family came first. I never sent it. Instead, I let him go, and I never saw him again."

She swallowed hard, her eyes burning with unshed tears. This was the part of her life no one had ever known. Not even David, her husband, who had loved her so deeply. He had given her a good life, and she had loved him in return, but the ghost of James had always lingered in the shadows of her heart.

"Your father and I built a beautiful life together," she continued, her voice steadying. "He was a good man, a man who loved me with all his heart. I never regretted marrying him, never doubted the life we shared. But I want you to understand that love is not always simple. Sometimes, we make sacrifices for the people we love, and those choices shape who we become. I made my choice to stay with my family, to build the life that you are all a part of now."

Margaret wiped away a tear, her gaze drifting to the fireplace where the flames danced quietly. The fire crackled, filling the room with warmth, yet her heart felt exposed, vulnerable in a way it hadn't in years. She had spent her life protecting her family, holding on to this secret to keep the peace. But now, she realized that the truth—however painful—was a gift. It was a part of her, and by sharing it, she was allowing her family to truly know her.

"I have held onto this secret for many years," she wrote, her hand steady now. "I did so because I wanted to protect all of you, to spare you from the complexities of my past. But I realize now that it's important for you to know the truth. Not because it changes anything, but because it is part of the story of who I am. A story that has shaped the woman you know as your mother, your grandmother."

She took a deep breath, feeling the weight lift from her chest as she poured the last of her heart onto the page.

"James was my first love, but your father was the love of my life. I chose him, I chose this family, and I have never regretted that choice. I only hope that in sharing this with you, you will understand that life is full of difficult decisions. Sometimes, we must sacrifice one dream to build another."

Margaret set the pen down, her fingers releasing the tension they had held. She leaned back in her chair, closing her eyes for a moment as a sense of peace settled over her. The truth was finally out, no longer a secret locked away in the quiet corners of her heart.

She glanced at the letter, still unfinished but somehow complete. The story had been told, and though she couldn't predict how her family would react, she felt a deep sense of relief. It was time to let go, to allow them to see her fully, flaws and all.

Margaret folded the letter carefully, slipping it into an envelope. The fire crackled softly beside her, and for the first time in years, she felt a lightness in her chest. The weight of her secret had been lifted, and with it came a quiet, comforting sense of closure.

MARGARET SEALED THE envelope with a steady hand, smoothing the edges with her fingers as if sealing away the last pieces of the burden she had carried for so long. The weight of her secret had been heavy, but now it felt distant, as if it no longer belonged to her alone.

She stood up from the desk, the ache in her knees reminding her of her age, and walked slowly to the window. Outside, the snowstorm had settled into a quiet, gentle snowfall, blanketing the world in a soft white glow. It was peaceful, and Margaret couldn't help but smile at the stillness of the scene. It reminded her of the calm she now felt inside—a quiet, comforting peace that had been absent for years.

The letter rested in her hand, light but full of the truth she had finally shared. Her eyes lingered on the envelope for a moment longer, as if saying goodbye to the part of herself she had kept hidden for so long.

She knew that once it was sent, there would be no taking it back. Her family would know everything, and she had no way of knowing how they would react. Would they understand? Would they see it as a betrayal of sorts, that she had kept something so important from them for all these years? Or would they see it for what it truly was—a testament to the complexity of life and love, to the choices she had made, not out of selfishness, but out of a desire to protect them?

Margaret's breath hitched slightly, but then she exhaled slowly, allowing herself to let go of the uncertainty. She had done what she needed to do. The truth was out now, and whatever came next was no longer in her hands.

With that thought, she walked to the door, pulling her warm coat from the hook and slipping on her boots. She tucked the letter into her bag, wrapping a scarf around her neck as she opened the door and stepped outside. The air was crisp and cold, but Margaret barely felt it. The snow crunched softly beneath her feet as she made her way down the path toward the mailbox at the end of the street.

The walk felt longer than usual, but not unpleasant. In the quiet of the evening, with the snow falling softly around her, Margaret felt a sense of clarity she hadn't felt in years. The world around her seemed brighter, more vivid, as if shedding the weight of her secret had made everything sharper, more real.

When she reached the mailbox, she hesitated for just a moment, her fingers resting on the cold metal of the handle. Then, with a small nod to herself, she opened it and slipped the letter inside, letting the flap close with a soft thud. It was done.

Margaret stood there for a few seconds longer, watching the snow fall, listening to the stillness around her. There was no turning back now, but she didn't feel afraid. Instead, she felt something she hadn't expected—comfort.

The truth was out, but so was her love, the love that had shaped every decision she had ever made. Her family, her children and grandchildren, would come to understand that, she hoped. But even if they didn't, she had given them the most honest part of herself, and that was enough.

As she turned and made her way back to the house, Margaret felt lighter, her steps easier. The house was warm and inviting when she stepped inside, the fire still crackling softly in the hearth. She hung up her coat and made her way to the living room, sitting down in her favorite chair by the fire.

The warmth of the flames wrapped around her like an embrace, and she closed her eyes, feeling a deep sense of contentment. The letter was out of her hands now, and so was the burden she had carried for so many years. She had told her story, and in doing so, she had set herself free.

Margaret didn't know what her family would say when they read the letter. She couldn't predict their reactions, but for the first time, that didn't matter. She had lived her life with love, with sacrifice, and now, with truth. Whatever came next, she would face it with the same quiet strength that had carried her through all these years.

As the fire crackled and the snow continued to fall outside, Margaret leaned back in her chair, feeling the warmth fill her home. For the first time in a long while, she felt at peace—truly, deeply at peace.

And that, she thought, was all she needed.

The Christmas Eve Stranger

The bell above the door chimed softly as Emily flicked off the lights of her bakery, leaving only the warm glow from the Christmas tree in the corner. She paused, surveying the space that had been her second home for years. The scent of cinnamon and freshly baked gingerbread still lingered in the air, a comforting reminder of the day's final rush of customers buying last-minute treats.

Outside, the snow had begun to fall heavily, blanketing the quiet streets of Pinebrook in a soft white hush. The town felt deserted now, with everyone tucked away in their homes, gathered around fireplaces and twinkling trees, while Emily remained alone, her hands wrapped around a warm mug of cocoa. The bakery had been her dream, her refuge. Yet on nights like these, when the world seemed to slow down and quiet wrapped around the town like the snow outside, she couldn't help but feel the hollow spaces that no amount of holiday cheer could fill.

Sighing, she walked to the window and peered out. The snowflakes swirled in the wind, almost dancing in the glow of the streetlights. Just as she turned away, there was a knock at the door—soft, hesitant. Emily froze, her heart skipping a beat. It was late, and no one should be out in a storm like this. She debated whether to answer, then slowly approached, pulling her cardigan tighter around herself.

Through the frosted glass, she could just make out the shadow of someone standing outside. With a quick inhale, she unlocked the door and opened it a crack. A gust of cold wind rushed in, and with it, the figure of a man bundled in a thick coat, his face partially hidden beneath a snow-dusted hat.

"Sorry to bother you," he said, his voice low and raspy, "but I saw the light. I... I just need somewhere to warm up for a bit. The storm—it's worse than I thought."

Emily hesitated, glancing over his shoulder at the swirling snow. He looked weary, his eyes dark but kind, the type of exhaustion that spoke of more than just a long walk in the cold. After a moment, she stepped aside. "Come in," she said softly, "before you freeze out there."

The stranger entered, shaking off the snow from his coat. His boots left wet prints on the floor as he took off his hat, revealing tousled hair streaked with silver. He offered a small smile of gratitude. "Thank you. I wasn't sure anyone would still be awake."

Emily shrugged, trying to mask her nervousness. "I was just closing up. It's not a night for anyone to be out."

The man nodded, his gaze wandering around the bakery, taking in the cozy decorations and the trays of leftover pastries that hadn't sold. "It's beautiful here," he said after a pause. "Feels like a place full of memories."

Emily gave a small, unsure smile. "It is, I suppose." She gestured toward a table by the window. "Would you like some tea? I've got a fresh pot."

"That would be wonderful," he said, settling into a chair with a grateful sigh.

As Emily moved to the kitchen to prepare the tea, she couldn't shake the odd sense of familiarity she felt. There was something about him—an air of sadness mixed with quiet calm—that tugged at her, as if she had known him in another life. She returned with a steaming cup, placing it in front of him, and sat across the table. For a while, they sipped in silence, the only sound the wind howling outside and the crackle of the bakery's small fireplace.

"You run this place by yourself?" the man asked after a while.

"Yeah," Emily nodded. "Been at it for almost seven years now. It's... a lot, but I love it."

He smiled softly, but there was something distant in his eyes. "Must be hard, though, especially on nights like this."

Emily studied him, sensing the weight of his words. "What about you? Where were you headed in this storm?"

The man hesitated, his fingers tracing the rim of his mug. "I was just... passing through. No real destination." He looked up, and in his gaze, Emily saw the depth of something she couldn't quite place—pain, loss, something hidden beneath the surface.

Emily leaned back in her chair, curiosity mixing with a sense of unease. "No destination?" she asked, her voice softer now. "That's a little unusual, don't you think? Especially on Christmas Eve."

The stranger gave a wry smile, his eyes never quite meeting hers. "Unusual seems to be a bit of a theme for me these days." He glanced out the window, where the storm was in full force, wind pushing snow against the glass. "I didn't expect the snow to get this bad, but I guess that's life for you—unexpected storms, changing everything in a blink."

There was a heaviness in his words, a hint of something deeper. Emily watched him closely, sensing the tension behind his calm exterior. She hesitated before speaking again. "If you don't mind me asking... what are you really running from?"

The stranger's smile faltered. For a long moment, he said nothing, staring down into his tea as if the answer might be hiding at the bottom of the cup. Finally, he spoke, his voice low and distant. "I wasn't always... like this. There was a time when I had everything—a family, a home, a life full of love. But I lost it. Slowly, piece by piece."

Emily's heart tightened, the warmth of the bakery contrasting sharply with the chill of his words. "Lost how?"

He sighed deeply, his breath almost shaking. "I was too focused on things that didn't matter. Work, success... I thought I had all the time in the world. But time... it slips away faster than you think. One day, I looked up and realized everything I cared about was gone. My wife, my kids—they grew tired of waiting for me to come back to them. And by the time I tried to fix things... it was too late."

Emily felt a pang in her chest. She didn't know this man, didn't know his life, but his story stirred something in her. A deep, familiar fear—the fear of losing what mattered most while chasing something that didn't.

"I'm so sorry," she said quietly, though the words felt inadequate.

The stranger shook his head. "Don't be. It's my fault. I made my choices, and I have to live with them. But that's the thing about regret—it sticks with you, no matter how far you go or how many miles you put between yourself and the past."

Emily shifted in her seat, her fingers wrapping around her mug. "Do you ever... think about going back? Trying again?"

His eyes, which had been so distant, flickered with a glimmer of something. Hope, maybe. Or just a fleeting thought. "I've thought about it every day for years. But some things... some bridges are burned too badly to rebuild."

The storm outside raged on, but the small space inside the bakery felt insulated, almost timeless. Emily's mind raced with thoughts of her own life—of the long days she spent in the bakery, the nights like this one where she went home alone, with only the quiet hum of the refrigerator for company. She had told herself this was enough, that the bakery filled her days and that she didn't need anything more. But hearing the stranger's story made her wonder if she was fooling herself. Was she, too, letting the things that mattered slip away without realizing it?

She glanced at the stranger, the sadness in his face reflecting something deeper in her own heart. "Maybe it's not too late," she said, her voice gentle but firm.

The man's brow furrowed slightly. "What do you mean?"

Emily leaned forward, her hands resting on the table between them. “Maybe you think you can’t go back. Maybe you’re afraid you’ll just make the same mistakes. But that doesn’t mean you shouldn’t try. Life’s short, like you said. Too short to live with regret.”

The stranger looked at her, really looked at her for the first time, as if her words had broken through some invisible wall he’d built around himself. His expression softened, and for a moment, Emily thought she saw something like gratitude in his eyes.

“Maybe,” he said, barely above a whisper. “Maybe you’re right.”

They sat in silence for a few minutes, the warmth of the bakery enveloping them both as the storm continued to rage outside. Finally, the stranger pushed his chair back and stood, brushing off his coat.

“I should let you close up,” he said, pulling his hat back over his head. “I’ve taken up enough of your time.”

Emily stood as well, reluctant to see him go, but unsure of what more she could say. “Are you sure you’ll be alright out there? The storm’s still pretty bad.”

The stranger smiled, a faint but genuine smile that transformed his face. “I’ll be fine. I think... I think I have some things I need to figure out.” He paused, his hand on the doorknob. “Thank you, Emily. For the warmth, the tea, and... the conversation. You’ve helped more than you know.”

Before she could respond, he stepped out into the swirling snow, the wind catching the door as it closed behind him. For a long moment, Emily stood there, staring at the empty street, her heart heavy but somehow lighter at the same time.

Emily stood frozen for a moment, watching the stranger’s silhouette fade into the snow before shaking herself back into the present. She quickly moved to the door, calling after him. “Wait! Please... stay. You don’t have to go out in this storm.”

The man hesitated, his figure faint through the thickening snow. After a beat, he turned and trudged back toward the bakery. Emily opened the door wider, the gust of wind sending a chill through the warm space. “You’ll catch your death out there,” she said, a half-smile tugging at her lips as she motioned for him to come back inside.

Once he was settled again, the warmth from the fire seemed to bring a flicker of color back to his pale face. Emily placed a plate of Christmas cookies on the table between them, the sweet scent filling the air. “I baked too many,” she said, almost apologetically. “You’d be doing me a favor by having some.”

The man smiled faintly, his eyes scanning the tray before taking a bite. “They’re good,” he murmured after a moment, the simple pleasure of food seeming to soften the edges of his weariness.

Emily poured more tea, the silence stretching between them, not uncomfortable but heavy with unsaid things. She could sense the storm within him, one that had little to do with the weather outside. After a few moments, he set his cup down, staring into it as though it held the answers to questions he hadn’t asked yet.

“I wasn’t always like this,” he began quietly, his voice low and rough, as if speaking these words cost him something. “There was a time when Christmas meant something. When life was... full.” His gaze lifted, meeting Emily’s eyes briefly before drifting away again. “I had a family. A wife. Two kids. We were happy. Or at least, I thought we were.”

Emily stayed silent, her hands resting on the warm mug, listening.

The man continued, his words slow, measured. “But I was always chasing something—success, I suppose. I spent so much time working, trying to provide, that I didn’t realize what I was losing in the process. I kept telling myself that I was doing it for them... but really, I think it was for me. I needed to feel like I was enough, and work was the only place I ever felt that.”

He paused, the weight of those memories hanging in the air. Emily could see the deep lines in his face, the burden of years lived in regret.

“They waited for me,” he said, his voice barely a whisper now. “For years, they waited for me to be present. To be there in more than just the physical sense. But I kept missing birthdays, holidays, moments I'll never get back. And one day... they were gone."

The silence that followed felt almost unbearable. Emily's heart ached for him, not because she knew him, but because his story felt universal—how easy it was to lose sight of what mattered, how fragile life could be. She shifted in her chair, unsure of what to say but feeling compelled to speak.

"I'm so sorry," she said softly. "That must have been—"

"Hard?" he finished for her, a bitter smile tugging at the corner of his mouth. "Yes, it was hard. But the hardest part wasn't losing them. It was realizing that I had done it to myself. I made those choices. I chose work over them, thinking there would always be time to fix it later."

He fell silent again, his eyes distant. "But there wasn't. And by the time I tried to make things right, they had moved on. I never got the chance to say I was sorry. Not really."

Emily swallowed, the lump in her throat growing. The storm outside seemed to have grown more ferocious, the wind howling against the windows. But here, in the bakery, the world felt smaller, more intimate. She didn't know this man, not really, but his story touched something deep inside her. She thought of her own life—how she'd poured everything into this bakery, telling herself it was enough, that it filled the empty spaces. But now, listening to him, she wasn't so sure.

"There's always a chance," Emily said, her voice gentle but firm. "Maybe it feels too late, but... you never know. People can surprise you. They might be waiting for you to come back, to try again."

The man looked at her, his expression softening as if her words had reached a part of him he thought was long dead. He said nothing for a long moment, his gaze holding hers as the fire crackled softly in the background.

"You really believe that?" he asked, his tone skeptical but not dismissive.

Emily nodded slowly. “I do. I’ve seen it happen. People reconnect after years apart, after mistakes, and somehow... they find their way back to each other.”

The stranger leaned back in his chair, his eyes flicking to the storm outside. “And what about you?” he asked quietly. “What are you waiting for?”

Emily blinked, surprised by the question. She hadn’t expected the conversation to turn back on her, but now that it had, she wasn’t sure how to answer. What was she waiting for? She had built this bakery, poured her heart and soul into it, but now, sitting here with this stranger, she realized that maybe she’d been hiding behind it. Maybe she, too, had been putting off what really mattered.

“I don’t know,” she admitted, her voice soft. “I guess I’ve been waiting for the right time. But... maybe there’s no such thing.”

The man nodded, a sad, knowing smile playing on his lips. “No,” he said quietly. “There usually isn’t.”

For a while, they sat in silence again, the storm outside louder now, howling with a fury that felt otherworldly. But inside the bakery, the warmth remained, wrapping around them both like a quiet promise.

The wind howled outside, shaking the windows as if the storm itself were alive, seeking entry. Inside, the heat from the fire warmed the bakery, but a different warmth filled the room—one that came from the conversation. Emily leaned forward slightly, her hands still cradling her mug. She could feel the weight of the moment, the invisible crossroad where they both stood.

The stranger’s gaze was fixed on the flickering flames. His face, once sharp with sorrow, had softened into a mask of quiet contemplation. The lines around his eyes spoke of years of regret, but now, there was a flicker of something else—an emotion he had kept buried for too long. Hope.

Emily cleared her throat, the sound breaking the silence between them. "You know," she began slowly, carefully choosing her words, "it's never too late to try."

He looked at her, his brow furrowing slightly. "You think after everything—after all these years—that they'd even want to see me again?"

She met his gaze, steady and unwavering. "I don't know them, and I don't know the whole story. But I do know people have a way of forgiving when they see someone truly trying. You said you never got the chance to apologize. Maybe that's what they've been waiting for."

The man's shoulders sagged, as if the thought weighed on him. He rubbed his hands together, staring into the fire again. "I left them," he murmured. "I let my pride keep me away for too long. I wouldn't even know where to begin."

Emily leaned back in her chair, drawing in a deep breath. She had thought about this moment carefully since the stranger had opened up about his past. His pain was palpable, but so was his desire for redemption. She couldn't let him leave without trying to guide him toward that path.

"You start by reaching out," she said, her voice gentle but firm. "You don't need a grand gesture. You don't need to show up with perfect words or elaborate apologies. Just start small. Call them, send a letter—even just to say you're sorry. Sometimes, it's the smallest acts that open the door."

He didn't respond right away, his face shadowed with doubt. Emily could see the war in his eyes—the pull of fear and pride that kept him from taking the first step. But she also saw the other side of him—the part that longed for peace, for a second chance to make things right.

"I've seen people wait too long," Emily continued, her voice quieter now, almost as if she were speaking to herself. "They convince themselves it's over, that it's too late. But life... it's unpredictable. We don't know how much time we have left to make amends. Don't wait for the perfect moment, because it might never come."

The man's eyes flickered toward her, searching her face. "You speak like you've lived through this yourself."

Emily smiled faintly, her gaze drifting toward the snow piling up outside the window. "In a way," she admitted. "I've lost people, too. People I thought I'd have more time with. And I didn't always get the chance to say what needed to be said." She paused, drawing in a breath. "That's why I'm telling you now... while you still have the chance."

He looked at her for a long moment, his expression unreadable. Then, slowly, his head dipped in a nod. "You're right," he said, his voice rough with emotion. "I've been running for so long, trying to avoid the pain, that I forgot the only way out is through."

Emily's heart lifted slightly. She hadn't known if her words would reach him, if he would take the advice she was offering. But seeing the flicker of resolve in his eyes, she felt a surge of quiet hope.

The fire crackled between them, and for a moment, the storm outside seemed distant, like the world had paused in this small, intimate space.

"I don't even know where to begin," he admitted, his voice softer now, vulnerable.

Emily smiled warmly. "Start by believing that it's possible. Sometimes, that's the hardest step. After that, everything else falls into place."

The stranger nodded again, his hands tightening around the mug as if holding onto something more than just the warmth it offered. He seemed lighter somehow, as though the weight of years had begun to lift, even if only slightly. He wasn't healed—far from it—but there was a seed of something new inside him now. The chance for redemption, the possibility of reconnecting with those he had lost.

Emily watched him, her own heart full. She had given him more than shelter from the storm—she had given him the chance to believe in second chances. And in doing so, she felt something shift within herself as well.

The storm outside raged on, but inside, there was peace. For the first time in a long time, Emily felt the warmth of hope stirring in her own soul.

When Emily awoke the next morning, the bakery was filled with soft light as the pale winter sun broke through the clouds. The storm had passed, leaving behind a pristine blanket of snow that glittered under the clear sky. It was as if the world had been washed clean, renewed after the harshness of the night.

Emily sat up in the small chair by the fireplace, realizing she must have dozed off after the stranger had gone to rest in the back room. The fire had long since died down, leaving only embers glowing faintly in the hearth. She stretched, feeling the stiffness in her muscles, but also the warmth in her heart from the conversation they had shared.

Rising to her feet, Emily moved toward the back of the bakery, expecting to find the stranger still resting. But when she reached the room, the bed was empty. His coat, hat, and shoes were gone, and there was no sign that anyone had been there at all. Her breath caught in her throat, and for a moment, she stood still, trying to process the quiet emptiness before her.

She hurried to the front door, pulling it open and stepping outside into the crisp morning air. The snow crunched softly under her boots as she looked around. The street was empty, the fresh snow undisturbed by any recent footprints. The stranger was gone.

Confused, Emily returned to the warmth of the bakery, her mind spinning. He must have left early, she reasoned. Perhaps the storm had cleared enough for him to continue on his way before dawn. But why hadn't he said goodbye? Had he truly found the resolve to seek out his family, or had he simply moved on without a word?

As she turned to close the door, something caught her eye on the counter beside the till. A small, folded piece of paper rested there, next to a delicate silver locket. Her breath caught as she approached, her fingers trembling slightly as she reached for the note.

The handwriting was simple and neat, the words few but meaningful:

"Thank you for showing me the way. I will find them."

Emily's eyes softened as she read the words, feeling a sense of relief and closure. The stranger had made his decision—he would seek redemption and reconnect with those he had lost. She touched the locket gently, flipping it over to reveal an engraving on the back. It was a single word: Hope.

The weight of the small token in her hand felt significant, as though it carried with it a message not only for him but for her as well. Emily closed her hand around the locket, holding it close to her heart. She wasn't sure if the man had been real or if he had been something more—an apparition sent to remind her of the power of kindness, forgiveness, and second chances.

Either way, she felt different. Lighter, somehow. The storm had been more than just a physical event—it had swept through her own heart, clearing away the remnants of her own regrets and uncertainties. In helping him find his way, she had found something within herself too—a renewed sense of purpose, a reminder of the importance of the simple, quiet gestures that could change someone's life.

The bell above the bakery door chimed softly as she turned to face the day. The streets outside were quiet and peaceful, but she knew that soon, the town would come alive with the sound of Christmas morning. Families would gather, children would laugh, and the spirit of the season would fill the air.

Emily smiled to herself, slipping the locket into her apron pocket. She had work to do—there were pastries to bake and people to greet. But now, as she moved through the familiar tasks of the morning, she carried with her the memory of the stranger and the reminder that, in the smallest moments, lives could be changed forever.

And though she might never see him again, she knew that wherever he was, he carried with him the hope she had offered. Perhaps, in some small way, she had been the one to give him a second chance.

The thought brought warmth to her chest, and as Emily prepared for the day ahead, she whispered softly to herself, “Merry Christmas.”

The Wishing Star

The town of Hollyridge was always beautiful during Christmas. Nestled in a valley surrounded by tall, snow-dusted pines, it looked as if it had leapt straight out of a painting. Cobblestone streets were lined with garlands and twinkling lights, while the scent of pine and cinnamon wafted through the air. The townsfolk bustled with last-minute shopping, their cheeks rosy from the cold, their hands full of wrapped presents and warm pastries.

But for all the festive cheer outside, Leo McAllister's house was quiet. It wasn't that his family didn't love Christmas—they did. But this year, things were different. Leo's father had lost his job at the mill a few months back, and his mother was working extra hours at the bakery just to keep the house warm. Money was tight, and Leo knew better than to ask for the things he wanted—like the shiny red toy train he'd seen in the shop window every day on his way to school.

As he sat by the window, staring at the Christmas decorations in the distance, Leo felt a knot form in his chest. His mind was always filled with wonder, with dreams of adventure, but this year felt heavier. He wanted to believe in something magical, something bigger than himself, but the weight of reality was starting to settle on his young shoulders.

"Leo," his mother called from the kitchen, "come help me with the cookies."

He jumped down from the windowsill and shuffled into the kitchen. The warm smell of gingerbread greeted him, but even that couldn't lift his spirits.

"Are we going to decorate them with sprinkles?" he asked, trying to sound cheerful.

His mother smiled, though her eyes looked tired. "Of course we are. They wouldn't be Christmas cookies without sprinkles, would they?"

Leo helped her roll out the dough, cut the gingerbread men, and carefully place them on the baking tray. But as they worked, his thoughts drifted. He thought about his friends at school, all of whom had been talking about the presents they hoped to find under the tree. He hadn't said anything when they asked him what he wanted. He knew that Christmas this year wasn't going to be about presents—not for him, at least.

Later that evening, after dinner, Leo bundled up in his coat and scarf and stepped outside. The snow had begun to fall again, softly at first, and the world seemed to quiet under its gentle blanket. He loved this time of night, when everything was still, and the stars seemed to shine brighter in the cold, crisp air.

He wandered down the street, his boots crunching in the fresh snow. As he walked, he glanced up at the sky, his breath coming out in small puffs of steam. The stars were scattered like diamonds across a velvet backdrop, twinkling in their distant, mysterious way. Leo had always been fascinated by the stars. They seemed like something from another world, full of secrets and stories that no one on Earth could ever know.

But tonight, one star stood out. It wasn't twinkling like the others. It was streaking across the sky, a bright, golden light cutting through the darkness. Leo's heart leapt as he watched it fall, his breath catching in his throat. He had heard of shooting stars before, but this one was different. It was bigger, brighter, and seemed to be falling...closer.

Without thinking, Leo began to run. His boots slipped on the icy street, but he didn't slow down. The star was heading toward the woods behind the town, a place he had played countless times with his friends. He knew the paths like the back of his hand.

As he reached the edge of the forest, the star disappeared behind the trees, and for a moment, the night seemed even darker. But Leo pressed on, his heart pounding in his chest. He weaved through the trees, the snow crunching under his feet. The deeper he went, the quieter the world became, until all he could hear was his own breathing and the soft whisper of the wind through the branches.

Then he saw it.

In a small clearing, nestled between the snow-covered pines, was the star. It lay on the ground, glowing softly, its light casting a warm golden hue on the surrounding snow. It wasn't like anything Leo had ever seen before. It wasn't just a ball of light; it was a perfect star-shaped crystal, about the size of his hand, and it pulsed gently, as if it were alive.

For a moment, Leo stood frozen, unsure of what to do. He had never expected to actually find it, let alone touch it. But something inside him told him to move closer. Slowly, he stepped forward, the warmth from the star chasing away the cold that had seeped into his bones.

His hand hovered over the star for a moment before he reached down and picked it up. The moment his fingers touched the crystal, he felt a strange sensation—like a rush of energy, a soft hum that seemed to fill the air around him. The star was warm in his hands, glowing brighter now that he held it.

Leo's mind raced. Could this really be what he thought it was? The legend his grandmother had told him when he was younger came flooding back: "If you ever find a star that falls from the sky, it can grant one wish. But remember, Leo, the wish must come from the heart. It must be selfless for it to work."

His heart raced as he thought about all the things he could wish for. The toy train...his father's job...new clothes for school. But then he stopped, staring down at the glowing star. The legend had been clear. The wish couldn't be for himself. It had to be selfless.

Leo stood in the clearing, his breath forming small clouds in the cold air, the star warm in his hands. The snow had begun to fall again, gently blanketing the ground, but Leo didn't notice. His thoughts were racing. A wish. A single, powerful wish.

He had never been one to believe in magic—not really. But here, in the quiet of the forest, holding a glowing star that had fallen from the sky, it was impossible not to. The star pulsed softly, as if waiting, as if listening.

The toy train came to his mind again—the shiny red one he had dreamed about since seeing it in the shop window. For a moment, Leo could almost see it: the little engine whirring down the tracks, the tiny passengers waving from the windows. He wanted it more than anything.

But then, his grandmother's words echoed in his mind once more: "It must be selfless for it to work."

Leo bit his lip. He knew what that meant, and it made his heart sink a little. This wasn't about getting what he wanted. It couldn't be.

He closed his eyes, thinking hard. Who needed this wish more than he did? His family came to mind first—his father, still searching for work; his mother, tired from long hours at the bakery. He could wish for his father to get a job again, for his mother to have less to worry about. That would be a good wish, right?

But even as he thought it, Leo hesitated. He knew his parents would want more than just good fortune for themselves. They'd want something bigger—something that could bring joy to others, too. And then Leo thought about the town.

Hollyridge had always been a close-knit place. Everyone knew everyone else, and they always looked out for one another. But this year had been tough for many families, not just his own. There had been layoffs, like the one that had taken his father's job, and several homes had lost power during the winter storms. Some of the older folks, like Mrs. Connors next door, had barely enough money to buy food, let alone presents.

As Leo stood in the snow, holding the star, the faces of his neighbors flashed through his mind—Mrs. Connors, who always gave him extra cookies when he helped shovel her walk; Mr. and Mrs. Sanderson, who owned the little grocery store and had given his family extra food when times were tough; even his friends at school, many of whom would be waking up to modest Christmas mornings, just like him.

The thought tugged at him, filling him with a strange kind of warmth that had nothing to do with the star in his hands. What if his wish could help all of them? What if he could bring happiness to everyone, not just his family, but the whole town? Was that even possible?

Leo looked down at the glowing star. It was still warm, still pulsing softly, as if it were waiting for him to make up his mind. He took a deep breath.

"I wish," he whispered, "I wish for everyone in Hollyridge to have a Christmas filled with happiness and warmth. I wish that no one will be lonely, and everyone will have what they need, even if it's just for one day."

The moment the words left his mouth, the star grew brighter, its light shining so intensely that Leo had to squint. He held it tightly, feeling the warmth spread from his hands all the way through his body, as if he were being wrapped in a cozy blanket.

Then, as quickly as it had begun, the light dimmed, and the star's glow softened. Leo blinked, looking around the clearing. Everything was still. The snow fell gently, and the trees stood tall and silent around him. For a moment, he wondered if anything had happened at all. Had the star truly granted his wish?

He tucked the star into his pocket, feeling its warmth through his coat, and made his way back through the forest, following the path he knew so well. The snow crunched under his feet, and as he reached the edge of the woods, he noticed something strange.

The town of Hollyridge, now visible through the trees, was...different. Lights shone brightly from every window, far more than he had seen earlier. The houses, once dark and quiet, now seemed alive with activity. Leo could hear the faint sound of laughter and music drifting on the night air. It was as if the entire town had woken up, filled with a new energy.

His heart raced as he hurried down the street, his boots sliding on the icy patches. As he passed Mrs. Connors' house, he saw her sitting by the window, a smile on her face, her small Christmas tree aglow with lights. Further down, the Sandersons' grocery store was open, even at this late hour, with a handful of neighbors gathered inside, sharing hot cocoa and warm conversation.

Leo couldn't believe it. The town felt...happy. The same kind of happiness he had wished for. People who had seemed weary and worried just hours ago were now smiling, laughing, and talking with one another. There was a sense of joy in the air, a kind of warmth that couldn't be measured by the fire in a hearth.

He made his way home, his heart full. When he opened the door, he found his parents sitting by the fire, their faces alight with joy. His mother, who had looked so tired earlier, was laughing with his father, who sat beside her, his arm around her shoulders. Leo noticed a small pile of presents under their modest tree—presents that hadn't been there before.

"Leo!" his mother called when she saw him. "Where have you been? You won't believe it! People from all over town have been dropping by, bringing gifts, food, everything we need for the holiday!"

Leo stood in the doorway, his hand still resting in his pocket where the star lay, now cool and still. He smiled at his parents, feeling a deep sense of contentment. The toy train no longer seemed important. Seeing the joy in his parents' faces, the happiness that had spread through the town—it was more than enough.

Christmas morning arrived with the sound of carolers in the streets and the smell of freshly baked bread wafting through the town. Leo woke up to find Hollyridge transformed. The people of the town had come together like never before, sharing what they had, ensuring that no one went without.

As he stepped outside into the snow, Leo felt something even more magical than a wish come true: he felt connected, not just to his family, but to his entire town. The warmth he had wished for was more than just the glow of a fire or the sparkle of Christmas lights. It was the warmth of giving, of selflessness, and of something greater than himself.

And as the snow fell softly around him, Leo looked up at the sky and smiled, knowing that sometimes, the greatest wishes were the ones made for others.

Christmas morning arrived with a bright sun that peeked over the snowy hills, casting a soft golden light across the town of Hollyridge. The snow that had blanketed everything the night before now sparkled like a sea of diamonds. The town, still buzzing from the unexpected joy of the night before, awoke to a peaceful yet magical feeling, as if the very air hummed with possibility.

Leo rubbed his eyes and stretched, his body still cocooned in the warmth of his blankets. He glanced around his small room and noticed something unusual: there, on his desk, was a small wooden box, delicately wrapped in shimmering silver paper. He hadn't seen it the night before, and he knew there had been no presents for him.

Curious, he climbed out of bed, his bare feet touching the cold wooden floor as he padded over to the desk. He ran his fingers over the smooth surface of the box and then carefully untied the silver ribbon. As he lifted the lid, he gasped. Inside was the train—the shiny red toy train he had longed for, the one he had dreamed about since the day he saw it in the shop window. Its miniature engine gleamed in the soft morning light, and beside it were two small passenger cars, each one painted with delicate detail.

For a moment, Leo stood frozen, his mind trying to catch up with what his eyes were seeing. How could this be? He had made his wish for the town, not for himself. And yet here it was—the very thing he had wanted most of all.

His heart swelled with gratitude, but it wasn't just for the train. It was for the realization that sometimes, when you give to others, the universe finds a way to give back to you in unexpected ways.

Leo's thoughts were interrupted by the sound of his mother's voice calling him from downstairs. "Leo! Breakfast is ready! Come down before it gets cold!"

He carefully placed the train back in its box, a smile tugging at the corners of his lips, and hurried down the stairs. His parents were already at the table, his father holding up a plate of warm pancakes, his mother pouring orange juice into glasses. The small tree in the corner of the room was surrounded by even more gifts, though they were modest, each one carefully wrapped with love.

"Morning, sleepyhead!" his father greeted him with a grin. "Did you see your present?"

Leo nodded, sliding into his seat. "I did. It's perfect."

His mother beamed, her face glowing with happiness. "I don't know how it got there," she said, "but it's exactly what you wanted, isn't it?"

Leo nodded again, his eyes sparkling. He didn't need to explain. Somehow, his family understood that this Christmas was different—special, in a way that went beyond the presents under the tree.

As they ate breakfast, the warmth in their small house felt brighter, more real. His father spoke of new job opportunities that had come to town, his mother talked about all the people who had stopped by the bakery with kindness and food to share. It was as if the whole community had been touched by something magical.

After breakfast, Leo bundled up in his coat and boots, and his parents waved him off with smiles as he headed outside. The streets of Hollyridge were alive with people—neighbors helping each other shovel snow, children playing with new sleds and toys, families exchanging hugs and laughter. The cold had no hold on their spirits.

As Leo walked through the streets, he found himself at the edge of the woods where he had discovered the fallen star the night before. He stood there for a moment, looking up at the sky, now a clear, brilliant blue. He wondered what had become of the star. Was it still hidden somewhere in the forest, or had it returned to the sky, its purpose fulfilled?

Just then, he heard a soft rustling from the trees behind him. He turned and saw an elderly man standing just a few paces away, leaning on a cane. The man's eyes twinkled, and his wrinkled face was lit with a kind smile.

"You've been busy, haven't you, young man?" the stranger said in a gentle, raspy voice.

Leo blinked in surprise. "Do I know you?" he asked, his voice quiet but curious.

The old man chuckled, his breath puffing out in small clouds. "In a way, yes. I've been watching over this town for a long, long time. It's rare to find a boy with a heart as pure as yours." He gestured toward the woods. "Not many would have made the wish you did."

Leo's eyes widened. "You know about the wish? About the star?"

The man nodded slowly. "I do. The star finds those who need it most—and more importantly, those who can use its magic selflessly." He looked at Leo with a glint of pride in his eyes. "And you did, Leo. You made a wish that wasn't for yourself, and because of that, you've given more than you can imagine."

Leo felt his cheeks flush, unsure of how to respond. "But... I didn't do much," he said, his voice small. "I just wanted everyone to be happy."

"And that," the man said softly, "is what makes it so powerful. Kindness, boy—real, unselfish kindness—is the greatest magic of all."

For a moment, the two stood in silence, the snow falling gently around them. Leo felt a strange sense of peace in the presence of the old man, as if he were standing with someone who had been a part of this place for longer than time itself.

"Will the star come back?" Leo asked, looking up at the sky again.

"Perhaps," the man said, smiling. "When the time is right, and when another like you is needed."

Leo nodded, feeling a sense of understanding settle over him. He glanced down at his pocket, where he still carried the now-dim star, and when he looked up again, the man was gone.

He stood alone at the edge of the forest, but he didn't feel lonely. Instead, he felt connected to something much bigger than himself—something timeless and full of wonder.

With one last look at the forest, Leo turned and headed back toward the town. The laughter and warmth of Hollyridge wrapped around him, and as he walked through the streets, he knew that this Christmas would be remembered not just for the gifts or the joy, but for the kindness that had spread through their little town like a blanket of snow.

And somewhere, far above, the stars twinkled in the bright winter sky, watching over them all.

As the day unfolded, Hollyridge seemed to shimmer with the kind of joy that can only be felt in the deepest parts of winter, when the cold outside is contrasted by the warmth of human connection. Families gathered around fireplaces, children played in the snow, and everyone exchanged small, thoughtful gifts that brought smiles to even the most weathered faces. The happiness that filled the town wasn't just from material things, though. There was something else, something that lingered in the air, like the faintest scent of pine and cinnamon, something magical.

Leo spent most of the morning helping his parents prepare Christmas dinner. The kitchen was filled with the smell of freshly baked bread, roasted vegetables, and his mother's famous cranberry sauce. Every so often, they paused to laugh, sharing memories from past holidays. His father, usually quiet and reserved, seemed lighter today, joking more often and even humming a Christmas tune as he carved the roast.

Despite the cheer surrounding him, Leo couldn't help but think back to his encounter with the old man by the forest. His words echoed in Leo's mind: "Kindness is the greatest magic of all." Leo had always believed in magic, but now he understood it was different from the fairy tales and stories he'd grown up with. Real magic, he realized, was the ability to change someone's life, even in the smallest of ways. And that's what his wish had done—not just for his family but for the whole town.

After dinner, Leo asked if he could go outside one last time before it got dark. His parents, still buzzing from the day's festivities, nodded with a smile, telling him not to stray too far. Bundling up in his coat and scarf, Leo stepped out into the crisp evening air. The sun was just beginning to set, casting long, golden shadows over the snow-covered streets. The town felt calm now, peaceful, as if it were resting after a day filled with joy.

Leo wandered through the streets, his boots crunching in the snow, until he found himself at the small town square. The large Christmas tree, now adorned with bright lights and hand-made ornaments, stood tall in the center, its star shining at the very top. Around it, families gathered to chat and laugh, their faces still glowing from the warmth of the holiday spirit.

Leo smiled as he watched them, feeling a deep sense of pride. He had wished for happiness and warmth, and now he could see it in every face he passed. People who hadn't spoken to each other in years were now exchanging smiles and greetings. Neighbors were helping one another clear snow from their steps, children were sharing their toys, and there was a sense of unity in the air that Hollyridge hadn't seen in a long time.

As he stood there, he noticed a small girl sitting alone on a bench at the edge of the square. She couldn't have been more than six or seven years old, bundled in a bright red coat with a matching scarf wrapped tightly around her neck. Her hands were cupped around a small snow globe, and she stared into it with a quiet intensity, as if lost in her own world.

Curious, Leo walked over and sat beside her. For a moment, neither of them spoke. They just sat there, watching as the lights from the Christmas tree reflected in the snow globe's glass dome.

"It's beautiful, isn't it?" Leo said softly, nodding toward the snow globe.

The girl looked up at him with wide, blue eyes. She smiled faintly and nodded. "It's my favorite," she whispered. "My grandma gave it to me last Christmas."

Leo smiled. "It's a good one. Do you shake it sometimes to make the snow fall?"

The girl nodded again, her fingers tracing the edge of the globe. "I do, but... I don't want to shake it too hard. I'm afraid it'll break."

Leo looked at her more closely. There was something sad in her voice, a heaviness that didn't seem to belong to someone so young. "Is your grandma coming to visit for Christmas?" he asked gently.

The girl shook her head. "She... she passed away last year," she said, her voice barely above a whisper. "This was the last present she gave me."

Leo's heart ached for the girl. He knew what it was like to miss someone so much it hurt, especially during the holidays. "I'm sorry," he said softly. "But you know what? As long as you remember her, she's still with you. In here." He pointed to his chest. "And in that snow globe, too."

The girl looked up at him, her eyes brightening a little. "You think so?"

"I know so," Leo said with a smile. "Love never really goes away. It just changes form."

They sat in silence for a few more moments, watching the snow begin to fall lightly around them. The girl shook her snow globe gently, watching as the tiny flakes swirled around the miniature Christmas tree inside.

"You're right," she said finally. "It does feel like she's still with me."

Leo nodded. "She is."

As the girl's father came to take her home, she waved goodbye to Leo, her face glowing with a new kind of warmth. Leo waved back, feeling a sense of peace settle over him. He had helped her, just as the old man had said—through kindness, he had brought a little more magic into the world.

The night was growing darker, and the town square was slowly emptying out as people returned to their homes. Leo stood up and began to walk back toward his house, his heart full. He had learned something important this Christmas. The real magic wasn't in the star, or even in the wish itself. It was in the act of giving, the selfless moments that made someone else's world a little brighter.

As Leo approached his house, he looked up at the night sky, where the stars twinkled faintly in the distance. He wondered if the star that had fallen was still out there, watching over him and his town. And then, for just a moment, he thought he saw one star, brighter than the others, wink at him from above.

With a smile, Leo stepped inside, knowing that the magic of Christmas wasn't just something you found in the sky—it was something you created with your heart.

And as he closed the door behind him, he whispered to the night, "Thank you."

The warmth of his home greeted Leo as he stepped inside, and the comforting sounds of his family chatting in the living room made him smile. His parents were sitting together on the couch, sipping hot cocoa and sharing stories about their own Christmas memories. The tree in the corner glowed softly, its lights twinkling like the stars outside.

Leo felt content, more than he ever had before. He'd learned the true meaning of Christmas, not through receiving but through giving, through thinking of others before himself. The star he'd found in the woods had taught him a lesson that no gift could replace.

As he approached his parents, his mother looked up at him, her eyes sparkling. "Where did you go, sweetheart?" she asked with a smile. "We missed you."

"I just needed to take a walk," Leo said, sitting down beside them. "I wanted to see the town, you know?"

His father nodded. "It's been a special day for all of us, hasn't it? There's something different this Christmas, something... magical."

Leo smiled softly. "Yeah, it really is different. It feels like everyone's just... happier."

His mother wrapped her arm around his shoulders, pulling him close. "And I think you had a lot to do with that, Leo. You've always had a big heart, and I'm proud of you."

Leo leaned into his mother's embrace, feeling the warmth of her love. He didn't need to tell her about the star or the wish. Somehow, he knew that the magic wasn't just in the act of wishing—it was in the change it had created in him, in the way he saw the world now.

As the evening wore on, Leo and his family gathered around the fireplace, sharing stories and laughter, the flicker of the flames casting a golden glow over the room. Outside, the snow continued to fall, blanketing the town in a peaceful silence.

Leo's thoughts wandered back to the star one last time. He had wished for happiness and warmth for his family and the people of Hollyridge, and now, as he looked around the room, he realized that his wish had come true. Not in the form of grand presents or extravagant gestures, but in the small, meaningful moments—the laughter shared, the kindness shown, the love felt between people.

And as the night deepened, Leo excused himself and went to his bedroom. There, by his window, he looked up at the sky once more. The stars were twinkling brightly, just as they had the night before. He felt a deep connection to them, as if the star he had found was still watching over him, reminding him of the power of selflessness.

Leo climbed into bed, pulling the blankets up to his chin. His heart was full, his mind at peace. As his eyelids grew heavy, he whispered into the quiet night, "Merry Christmas."

Outside, the snow fell in soft, delicate flakes, blanketing the town of Hollyridge in a quiet, magical stillness. And somewhere in the vast, starry sky, a single star shone just a little brighter, as if acknowledging the boy who had learned that the greatest gift of all wasn't something you could hold in your hands—but something you could give to others from your heart.

Leo drifted off to sleep with a smile on his face, knowing that this Christmas would be one he would never forget. It wasn't the presents or the decorations that made it special, but the simple magic of kindness, of thinking beyond oneself, and of believing in something greater.

And so, the legend of the wishing star lived on, not just in stories told by old men in the woods, but in the hearts of those who, like Leo, had learned the true meaning of Christmas.

The Nutcracker's Secret

Snowflakes drifted softly outside the window, a delicate dusting of white settling over the quiet street. Inside the house, Clara worked her way through a box of old ornaments, carefully untangling strings of twinkling lights and hanging them across the mantel. The Christmas tree stood tall in the corner, half-dressed in its usual array of ornaments, but Clara's attention had begun to wander.

She paused, running her fingers over the surface of an old, ornate Nutcracker sitting on the table beside her. It was a wooden figure, painted in rich reds and golds, its soldier-like stance both stiff and endearing. The Nutcracker had been her grandmother's favorite—a piece she always made sure was placed prominently under the tree each year. This Christmas, however, it had come to Clara, left to her in her grandmother's will just a few short months ago.

Clara sighed softly, the memory of her grandmother's warm laughter and the scent of her spiced cookies filling her mind. The Nutcracker felt like a connection to the woman she missed so much, a piece of the past that she was determined to cherish. She had never understood why her grandmother was so attached to the Nutcracker, but now that it belonged to her, she felt an odd pull toward it, as though it held more than mere sentimental value.

"Are you watching over me, Grandma?" Clara whispered, smiling to herself as she held the figure closer. The house was quiet, save for the crackling of the fireplace and the gentle hum of Christmas carols on the radio. It was peaceful—almost too peaceful, as if something just beyond her reach was waiting to be discovered.

With a final glance at the half-decorated tree, Clara sat down on the rug, cross-legged, and cradled the Nutcracker in her lap. She ran her hand over its polished wood, admiring the delicate craftsmanship. She'd held it many times before, but this time, something felt different.

As she turned it in her hands, she noticed a faint seam running along the Nutcracker's back. Clara frowned. She had never seen that before. Gingerly, she pressed against the seam, her curiosity getting the better of her. To her surprise, the back of the Nutcracker popped open with a quiet click. Inside, nestled carefully within a small compartment, was something unexpected—an old, yellowed piece of parchment and a tiny brass key.

Clara's breath caught in her throat. The key was shaped like a snowflake, its edges intricate and glimmering faintly in the firelight. Her heart raced as she unfolded the parchment, revealing a hand-drawn map, its lines fading with age but still legible. It didn't look like any place she recognized—there were strange landmarks, winding paths, and symbols she couldn't decipher.

She sat there for a moment, stunned. What was this? Why had her grandmother hidden it inside the Nutcracker? And why had she left it for Clara to find?

Questions swirled in her mind, but one thing was certain: whatever the map led to, it was meant for her to follow.

Inciting Event:

Clara sat frozen, her fingers tracing the edges of the old map, her mind racing. A part of her felt hesitant, unsure of what to make of it, but another part—a stronger, more curious part—urged her to continue. The map wasn't just an ordinary relic. It had been hidden, locked away, and kept secret for years. Her grandmother had left it for her to find, and that meant something important, perhaps even magical, lay ahead.

Clara turned the Nutcracker in her hands again, her eyes falling on the tiny key that had been tucked inside with the map. Its intricate snowflake design shimmered as though it, too, held secrets of its own. Without thinking much, she slipped the key into her pocket, folded the map carefully, and stood.

"I have to follow this," she whispered to herself, her heartbeat quickening with a mix of excitement and trepidation. She glanced at the clock on the wall—there was still time before dinner, plenty of time to explore. But where to start?

She studied the map more closely, looking for any clues. There was a small marking near the bottom of the parchment—an "X" next to an oddly familiar-looking tree. Clara squinted at it, and then it clicked. The tree wasn't just any tree. It was the old oak that stood in her grandmother's backyard, the one that had been there for as long as Clara could remember, with its gnarled branches stretching toward the sky like ancient arms.

Excitement welled up inside her, and before she could overthink it, Clara threw on her coat and boots and hurried outside. The cold winter air nipped at her cheeks, but she barely noticed as she crossed the yard, her gaze fixed on the towering oak. Snow crunched under her feet, the world around her still and silent, as if nature itself was holding its breath, waiting for her to take the next step.

She reached the base of the tree, and her eyes scanned its trunk, looking for something—anything—that might match the map. Her breath fogged in the air as she knelt down, brushing snow away from the ground. And then she saw it. A small notch carved into the bark, barely noticeable unless you were looking for it. It was the same snowflake shape as the key in her pocket.

With shaking hands, Clara pulled out the key and fit it into the notch. For a moment, nothing happened, and then, with a soft rumble, the earth beneath the tree shifted. Clara stumbled backward as a hidden door creaked open at the base of the oak. A cold draft escaped from the darkness below, carrying with it a faint scent of pine and something else—something older, almost like forgotten magic.

Clara hesitated for only a second before taking a deep breath and stepping inside. The stone staircase beneath the tree spiraled down into the earth, dimly lit by tiny glowing orbs that hovered just above her head. As she descended, the air grew warmer, the magic around her almost tangible. The weight of the Nutcracker in her arms felt heavier now, as though it too was coming alive with the secrets of this hidden place.

At the bottom of the stairs, Clara emerged into a cavernous room. Her eyes widened in wonder. Before her stretched an underground realm that seemed to glow with its own light—a forest of glittering trees, their leaves shimmering with gold and silver, streams of light cascading down like waterfalls in the distance. This was no ordinary place. It was as though she had stepped into a forgotten world, one that had been waiting for her.

And in the center of it all stood an old stone pedestal, upon which sat an ancient book, its pages worn but brimming with enchantment. Clara approached it cautiously, her heart pounding as she reached for the book. Her fingers brushed the cover, and with a soft hum, the pages flipped open on their own.

Words written in her grandmother's handwriting filled the first page:

"To my dearest Clara,

If you are reading this, then you've found what our family has long protected. This realm is tied to our past, to the very heart of our lineage. But dark forces threaten it once again, and now it falls to you, my brave girl, to finish what we started. Trust in the Nutcracker, for its power is greater than you know. Follow the map, and remember—you are never alone in this."

Clara's breath caught in her throat. The Nutcracker's secret wasn't just a hidden map. It was a key to this magical world, a world her family had once protected. And now, with her grandmother gone, the responsibility had fallen to her.

CLARA STOOD STILL, her mind spinning with the revelation. Her grandmother had protected this realm? And now, that burden rested on her? She looked down at the Nutcracker, cradled in her arms, feeling a strange warmth from it that she hadn't noticed before. It was as if the Nutcracker was trying to speak to her, urging her to move forward. But how? She felt unprepared, overwhelmed even.

Taking a deep breath, Clara read the note again, her grandmother's words echoing in her mind: Trust in the Nutcracker. Its power is greater than you know.

The Nutcracker's power... But what power? It was just a wooden figure, wasn't it?

Clara closed the book, tucking it under her arm as she stepped away from the pedestal. She surveyed the glowing forest before her. The shimmering trees, the light cascading like water—it was all mesmerizing. But behind the beauty, there was a faint tension in the air, a sense of unease that crawled up her spine. This magical world, once protected by her family, was now in danger.

As she pondered her next move, a rustling sound came from behind the trees. Clara's heart leapt in her chest. She instinctively clutched the Nutcracker closer, backing away. From the shadows emerged a small creature, its eyes wide and curious. It looked like a mix between a rabbit and a fox, with silver fur that shimmered in the light.

"Who are you?" Clara asked, her voice trembling.

The creature tilted its head, then spoke in a soft, musical voice. "I am Thistle, a guardian of the forest." It glanced at the Nutcracker in her arms, its eyes softening. "You carry the heirloom of protection. Your grandmother once wielded it."

Clara blinked in surprise. "My grandmother? What do you mean?"

Thistle approached her cautiously, its steps light on the forest floor. "Long ago, your grandmother and her ancestors watched over this realm. They were chosen to guard the balance between light and dark. But since her passing, the realm has been vulnerable. The dark force has awakened, growing stronger each day."

Clara's mind raced. Her grandmother had never mentioned any of this—no tales of magical realms or battles between light and dark. And yet, as she stood here, surrounded by an ancient forest glowing with enchantment, it all made sense in a strange way. The Nutcracker wasn't just a cherished ornament; it was part of her family's legacy, a symbol of protection for this realm.

"I didn't know," Clara admitted, her voice quiet. "I don't know what I'm supposed to do."

Thistle's eyes gleamed with compassion. "The Nutcracker has a power that can restore the balance. But you must discover how to unlock it. And you won't be alone." The creature motioned toward the trees, where more guardians began to emerge—small, glowing creatures with wings, silver foxes, and even a majestic stag whose antlers sparkled like ice.

Clara's chest tightened with a mix of fear and responsibility. She had never imagined herself in this kind of role. But her grandmother's words echoed in her mind—Trust in the Nutcracker.

"Where is this dark force?" Clara asked, her voice steadying as she spoke. "And how do I stop it?"

Thistle's expression grew serious. "The darkness has taken hold of the Hollow Keep, the heart of this realm. It was once a place of light and life, but now it is shrouded in shadows. The dark force seeks to consume the realm, to extinguish all the magic and wonder within it."

Clara gripped the Nutcracker tighter. "How do I get there?"

"The map will guide you," Thistle replied, nodding toward the parchment still clutched in her hand. "But be warned—dark creatures guard the Hollow Keep, and they will do everything in their power to stop you."

A chill ran down Clara's spine, but she squared her shoulders. This was her family's legacy. She couldn't turn away now, not when the realm needed her.

She unfolded the map again, scanning its ancient lines. The path to the Hollow Keep wound through dense forests, across frozen rivers, and up treacherous mountains. It was a daunting journey, but Clara knew she had to go.

"Let's go," she said, her voice firmer now, filled with resolve. "I'm ready."

Thistle smiled softly, and the other guardians stepped forward, surrounding her like a protective army. Clara felt a surge of courage. She wasn't alone in this. With the Nutcracker in her hands and the guardians by her side, she would face whatever danger lay ahead.

As they set off toward the Hollow Keep, Clara could feel the Nutcracker growing warmer in her hands. There was power within it—she just needed to figure out how to unlock it. And she had a feeling that the answer lay ahead, waiting for her in the heart of the shadows.

The journey to the Hollow Keep was even more perilous than Clara had imagined. The further she went, the darker the landscape became. The once vibrant trees were now twisted and bare, their branches clawing at the sky. Shadows seemed to stretch unnaturally long, creeping toward her as though alive. The guardians surrounding her grew tense, their once-glowing forms dimming as they moved deeper into the realm.

Clara held the Nutcracker close, feeling its warmth in contrast to the cold, biting air. Thistle led the way, navigating through the treacherous terrain with swift, silent steps. "We're close," he whispered, his voice barely audible above the eerie wind that whistled through the barren trees.

Suddenly, a deep rumbling shook the ground. Clara stumbled, grabbing onto Thistle for balance. "What was that?" she asked, her heart pounding in her chest.

"The dark creatures," Thistle replied, his eyes narrowing as he scanned the area. "They've sensed us. We must hurry."

They quickened their pace, but the rumbling grew louder, closer. Then, from the shadows, figures began to emerge—creatures made of darkness itself, with glowing red eyes and twisted forms. They moved like smoke, slithering and shifting, their presence cold and menacing.

Clara's pulse quickened. She could feel the weight of the Nutcracker in her hands, as if it were urging her to act. But how? What power did it hold?

One of the shadow creatures lunged toward her, its clawed hand reaching out. Clara instinctively raised the Nutcracker in front of her, and to her astonishment, a brilliant light erupted from it. The creature hissed, recoiling from the brightness, and the other creatures paused, wary of the Nutcracker's sudden glow.

Thistle's eyes widened. "The Nutcracker's power," he whispered. "It can drive them back."

Clara swallowed hard, realizing that the Nutcracker was more than just a key—it was a weapon. A weapon against the darkness.

With newfound courage, Clara stepped forward, holding the Nutcracker high. The light from it grew brighter, pushing back the shadows. The dark creatures screeched, retreating into the depths of the forest, but Clara knew they would return. They were only buying time.

"Come on!" Clara shouted, leading the way toward the towering silhouette of the Hollow Keep, its dark spires piercing the sky. The path grew steeper, and the air colder, but Clara's resolve only strengthened. The Nutcracker's light flickered slightly in her hands, but she held it tight, trusting in its power.

They reached the gates of the Hollow Keep, which were blackened and crumbling, covered in thick vines of shadow. Clara could feel the dark force pulsing from within, a heavy, oppressive energy that made it hard to breathe. But there was no turning back now.

With trembling hands, Clara stepped forward, placing the Nutcracker against the gate. For a moment, nothing happened. Then, the Nutcracker's light flared once more, and the gates groaned open, releasing a wave of cold air and darkness.

Inside, the Hollow Keep was even more foreboding. The walls were made of jagged stone, and the shadows clung to every corner like living things. At the center of the room stood a massive throne, and seated upon it was the source of the dark force—a figure cloaked in shadow, its form shifting and writhing like smoke.

The figure's eyes glowed red, locking onto Clara. "So, the last of the protectors has come," it hissed, its voice a low, guttural growl. "Your grandmother failed, and so will you."

Clara's heart pounded in her chest, but she forced herself to stay calm. She glanced at the Nutcracker, its light flickering but still strong. She had to trust in it, just as her grandmother had said.

"I won't fail," Clara said, her voice steady. "I'm not alone."

At her words, Thistle and the other guardians moved to her side, their eyes glowing with determination. The dark figure rose from the throne, its form growing larger, more menacing.

"You cannot defeat me," it growled, stretching out a hand toward Clara. Tendrils of darkness shot toward her, but Clara raised the Nutcracker, and once again, its light blazed. The darkness recoiled, but this time it didn't retreat completely. The force was too strong, and Clara could feel the Nutcracker's power waning.

She needed to unlock its full potential, but how?

In that moment, a memory flashed in her mind—her grandmother, sitting by the fire, telling her stories about the Nutcracker. It's more than just a toy, Clara. It's a symbol of protection, of courage, of love.

Clara's breath caught. Love. That was the key.

Her grandmother's love for this realm, for her family, for Clara—it was all tied to the Nutcracker's power. Clara closed her eyes, focusing on that love, letting it fill her heart. She thought of her grandmother, of all the times they'd shared, of the love that still connected them, even now.

The Nutcracker grew warm in her hands, and when Clara opened her eyes, its light was blinding, filling the entire room. The dark figure screamed, writhing in agony as the light pierced through it, dissolving the shadows bit by bit.

Clara stepped forward, her heart filled with love and courage. "You won't take this realm," she said firmly. "Not while I'm here."

With one final surge of light, the Nutcracker's power overwhelmed the darkness. The figure let out one last, ear-splitting scream before it disintegrated into nothingness, leaving the room bathed in a soft, golden glow.

The battle was over. Clara had won.

THE AIR IN THE HOLLOW Keep grew still, the oppressive weight of the darkness lifting at last. Clara stood in the center of the throne room, her chest rising and falling with each breath, the Nutcracker glowing softly in her hands. Around her, the guardians' forms shimmered in the golden light, their expressions relieved and proud.

Thistle approached her, his eyes glistening. "You've done it, Clara. The realm is safe."

Clara let out a shaky breath, the reality of what had just happened settling in. "I couldn't have done it without all of you," she said, glancing around at the guardians who had fought alongside her.

She looked down at the Nutcracker, now quiet and still, its power no longer burning brightly but resting peacefully. The intricate carvings on its surface seemed almost to smile, as if it too knew the realm had been saved.

"I didn't know my family had such a history," Clara said softly, her voice filled with wonder. "My grandmother... she was a protector, just like me."

Thistle nodded. "Your grandmother was one of the bravest protectors this realm has ever known. She kept the Nutcracker's secret for years, waiting for the right moment to pass it on to you. She believed in you, Clara. And now, you've proven her faith was not misplaced."

Clara's heart swelled with warmth at the thought of her grandmother, her presence now feeling even closer. "I miss her," she whispered, tears welling in her eyes. "But I know she's still with me, isn't she?"

Thistle smiled kindly. "She is. And as long as you carry the Nutcracker's legacy with love and courage, she'll always be by your side."

Clara nodded, wiping her eyes. "I'll protect this realm, just like she did. I'll make sure it stays safe."

With the darkness defeated and the realm at peace, the guardians guided Clara back to the portal that would lead her home. As she stepped through the shimmering veil of magic, she cast one last glance at the magical world her family had protected for so long. It felt bittersweet to leave, but Clara knew her journey wasn't truly over—it had only just begun.

In an instant, Clara found herself back in her living room, the warmth of the fireplace crackling in the background and the faint scent of pine filling the air. The Christmas decorations twinkled around her, just as she had left them, and snow gently fell outside the window.

She stood there for a moment, taking it all in. The house felt the same, yet Clara felt different—stronger, braver, as if the weight of her family's legacy now rested comfortably on her shoulders. She glanced down at the Nutcracker, now resting peacefully in her hands, and smiled.

Carefully, Clara placed the Nutcracker on the mantle, its rightful place among the other decorations. It was no longer just an heirloom—it was a symbol of her grandmother's love, of her family's courage, and of the magical world she now knew existed just beyond the surface of her own.

As she stepped back to admire the Nutcracker in the soft glow of the Christmas lights, Clara felt a deep sense of peace settle over her. She knew that her grandmother's spirit would always be with her, guiding her just as it had during her journey to the magical realm.

From that day forward, Clara kept the Nutcracker safe, treasuring its secret and the adventure it had brought into her life. She understood now that Christmas wasn't just about decorations and gifts—it was about family, legacy, and the magic that lives in all of us.

And every year, as the snow began to fall and the Nutcracker took its place on the mantle, Clara would remember the incredible journey she had taken, and the magical realm her family had once protected. She knew that one day, when the time was right, the Nutcracker's secret would be passed on again, and its magic would live on through future generations.

For now, though, Clara was content knowing that she had become part of something much bigger than herself—a family legacy filled with love, bravery, and the timeless magic of Christmas.

A Christmas Miracle on Maple Street

MAPLE STREET, ONCE bustling with laughter and life, now stood eerily quiet under a thick blanket of snow. The small town had fallen on hard times. With Christmas just days away, the joy that usually filled the air seemed to have vanished, replaced by the weight of unspoken worries.

At the corner bakery, Mrs. Thompson barely had enough customers to keep the doors open. Her hands, once busy crafting gingerbread houses and cinnamon rolls, now trembled with anxiety as she stared at unsold pastries. Across the street, Mr. Miller's hardware store, which had served the town for decades, faced the same fate—its shelves were full, but the shop was empty.

Families struggled too. The Petersons, who lived in the small house with the green shutters, were trying to stretch their last bit of savings to make Christmas special for their children. The sound of their kids' laughter had faded as presents became a distant dream. The holiday spirit had dimmed across the town, and hope seemed out of reach.

People passed each other on the street, heads low, nodding politely but without their usual warmth. The Christmas lights that once twinkled brightly now hung half-heartedly, their glow muted by the gloom of uncertainty. Maple Street, which had always been the heart of the town, was no longer beating with its usual joy.

The entire town felt this weight, like a shared burden no one knew how to lift. And as the snow continued to fall, the people of Maple

Street wondered if Christmas would pass them by this year, like a distant memory they could no longer grasp.

THE WIND HOWLED THROUGH the narrow streets of Maple Street, carrying with it whispers of an impending storm. As residents huddled in their homes, trying to find warmth in their small fires and worn blankets, the arrival of a stranger went unnoticed at first.

One morning, as dawn barely stretched its light across the snow-covered town, a man appeared at the edge of Maple Street. He was old, his face weathered and lined, with a beard that flowed like freshly fallen snow. His clothes, though simple and well-worn, were neat and clean, and he carried a large burlap sack slung over his shoulder. No one knew where he had come from—there had been no cars, no sleighs, and not even the distant sound of footsteps in the snow.

He began his slow, deliberate walk down Maple Street. His pace was unhurried, and his eyes, though kind, seemed to observe everything with a quiet understanding. Some noticed him as they peered from behind frost-covered windows, but no one approached. There was something mysterious about the man, something that made them pause.

The first to meet him was young Timmy Peterson. The boy, bundled up in layers of mismatched clothing, had been sent by his mother to pick up a loaf of bread from Mrs. Thompson's bakery. As Timmy trudged through the snow, kicking at ice patches to amuse himself, the stranger stopped him with a gentle wave.

"Good morning, lad," the old man said, his voice low but warm.

Timmy hesitated, unsure if he should respond, but there was something kind in the man's eyes. "Morning, sir," Timmy replied, shuffling his feet.

The old man reached into his burlap sack and pulled out a small wooden toy—a carved horse, no bigger than Timmy's palm, its craftsmanship intricate and beautiful. "For you," the man said, placing it gently in Timmy's hand.

Timmy stared at the toy in surprise. "But... I don't have any money," he stammered, looking up at the man.

The stranger smiled softly. "It's a gift, my boy. A little something to remind you that even small things can bring joy." With a wink, he continued on his way, leaving Timmy staring after him in awe.

By the time Timmy returned home, clutching the toy horse tightly, news of the old man had begun to spread. Mrs. Thompson, who had been sweeping the bakery steps in the cold morning air, had seen him next. He had stopped by her bakery, where shelves were still lined with unsold pastries, and handed her a small tin box, no bigger than her palm.

"It's nothing special, just something to hold your pennies," he had said with a twinkle in his eye. Mrs. Thompson had thanked him, though she couldn't understand why he would give her such a thing. When she opened the box later that afternoon, she found a single silver coin inside, glistening brightly under the light. The sight of it filled her with a strange, unexpected hope.

The old man continued his walk, stopping here and there along Maple Street. He gave Mr. Miller, the hardware store owner, a length of fine, old-fashioned rope, though Mr. Miller could not fathom its purpose. To the frail widow, Mrs. Jenkins, he offered a pair of woolen mittens, and to the schoolteacher, Miss Parker, a simple leather-bound notebook.

Each gift was small, almost too small to seem significant. Yet there was something about the way the old man gave them—something in his eyes, his smile, and the gentle manner in which he spoke—that left the recipients with a strange sense of comfort.

At first, the townspeople thought little of these gifts. After all, what use was a toy horse, a tin box, or a piece of rope when the town itself was crumbling under the weight of financial hardship? But as the day wore on, small miracles began to unfold.

Mrs. Thompson, after placing the silver coin in her cash register, saw a group of customers wander into her bakery—people she hadn't seen in months. By evening, she had sold out of nearly everything, her shelves bare for the first time in what felt like years. She wiped her brow in disbelief, smiling for the first time in weeks.

Mr. Miller, puzzled by the gift of rope, hung it in his shop as decoration. Later that afternoon, a young couple, new to town, came in, drawn by the sight of the shop's simple yet nostalgic display. They spoke to him at length, and by the end of their conversation, they had purchased enough supplies to start renovations on their new home. The sale was enough to keep Mr. Miller's store open through the new year.

And young Timmy, who had spent hours playing with his wooden toy horse, unknowingly lifted the spirits of his entire family. His laughter, which had been missing for so long, filled the Peterson household once more, bringing a warmth that had been absent in their small home for far too long. The simple joy of his playing seemed to remind them of something they had forgotten—something about the magic of Christmas.

Word of the old man and his strange gifts spread quickly. People began to whisper about him, wondering who he was and what he wanted. Some speculated he was a traveler from a distant land, while others believed he might be one of those eccentric types who drifted from town to town. But no one could explain the curious changes happening in Maple Street, the way it felt as though the air itself was lighter, filled with something new and hopeful.

The old man himself had disappeared into the snowy landscape, but his presence lingered in the hearts of the townspeople. They began to look at each other differently—no longer as strangers bound by their own problems, but as neighbors. A new spirit started to grow on Maple Street, fragile but undeniably real.

And so, with the snow falling softly, something extraordinary was beginning to happen in the small town. The people, once weighed down by their troubles, began to believe in something greater, though they couldn't quite name it yet. Something was shifting, like the first flicker of a flame ready to burst into light.

As the days passed, the mysterious old man vanished from Maple Street just as quietly as he had appeared, but the effect of his gifts lingered. Maple Street, once buried under the weight of despair, began to stir with life. The small tokens he left behind sparked something within the townspeople, and a change spread like a ripple across the town.

Mrs. Thompson's bakery, which had been on the brink of closing, was now bustling with customers each morning. Word had spread about her cinnamon rolls, and people from neighboring towns began to visit. Mrs. Thompson, who had once worried about how she would keep her doors open, now found herself waking up early each morning with a renewed sense of purpose. Her hands, once trembling with fear, were steady again, kneading dough and frosting cookies with the same joy she had when she first opened the shop years ago.

The transformation wasn't limited to the bakery. Mr. Miller's hardware store, which had seemed doomed just a week earlier, now buzzed with the sound of customers browsing, discussing plans for home repairs, and laughing with one another. The old rope that the man had given Mr. Miller became a curious focal point. People would stop in, asking about it, and end up purchasing tools or supplies. Mr. Miller had no explanation for the sudden interest but was grateful. For the first time in months, he had hope that his shop would survive.

The real magic, however, was not in the individual businesses recovering—it was in the way the people of Maple Street began to help one another. It started with small gestures. One evening, Mrs. Jenkins, the elderly widow who had received the woolen mittens, found a basket of groceries left on her doorstep. No note, no explanation—just a simple act of kindness. The next day, she made extra soup and shared it with her neighbors, something she hadn't done in years.

Timmy Peterson's father, once too weighed down by his own financial struggles to consider others, fixed the fence of the Jenkins' home without being asked. Miss Parker, the schoolteacher, started organizing after-school activities for the children, filling their afternoons with crafts, songs, and holiday decorations. The children's laughter, which had been absent for so long, now rang through the streets.

The gifts the old man had left seemed to have awakened a spirit of generosity. People who had barely spoken to one another before now stopped on the street to chat, to offer help, or simply to share a smile. The town's Christmas decorations, which had hung half-heartedly, were now being repaired and added to by the townspeople themselves. Families worked together to string lights from house to house, and soon, Maple Street was aglow with festive colors. The snow, once a reminder of cold and hardship, now sparkled under the light as if reflecting the warmth that had returned to the town.

One afternoon, just a few days before Christmas, a group of children gathered at the town square to build a snowman. Their laughter was infectious, and soon the adults joined in, helping them gather snow and find the perfect scarf and hat. Even those who had been feeling the sting of loneliness—like Mr. Jenkins, whose wife had passed the previous year—found themselves smiling, drawn into the community's renewed sense of togetherness.

And then, as if inspired by the old man's example, the townspeople began to exchange their own small gifts with one another. A batch of cookies left on a doorstep, a warm blanket delivered to someone in need, an extra load of firewood stacked outside a neighbor's house—none of these acts were grand, but they added up, creating a wave of goodwill that spread through every corner of Maple Street.

The town, once dimmed by hardship, now shimmered with light—not just from the decorations, but from something deeper. The spirit of Christmas had returned, not through extravagant gifts or grand gestures, but through simple acts of kindness and generosity.

Still, as the days drew closer to Christmas, there was a sense of anticipation. The townspeople couldn't shake the feeling that the old man had left them with more than just material gifts. It was as if he had planted a seed, and they were waiting to see what it would grow into.

Then, on the night before Christmas Eve, a letter appeared in the center of town, tacked to the community bulletin board. The townspeople gathered around it, curious, as the snow gently fell. The letter was written in elegant, old-fashioned script, and it simply read:

"To the people of Maple Street,

You have found the true gift of Christmas in each other. In the warmth of your hearts, the light of your kindness, and the strength of your togetherness, you have created something far more precious than any gift I could give you.

But I have one last gift to offer—this time, a gift from all of you. Together, you have the power to create your own Christmas miracle.

With love and gratitude,

An old friend."

The townspeople stood in silence, staring at the letter. They knew, without having to say it, that the old man had been much more than a passing stranger. He had come to remind them of something they had forgotten—that the true spirit of Christmas wasn't in gifts or decorations but in the love and kindness they shared with one another.

Suddenly, a wave of ideas began to flow. People spoke excitedly about how they could make this Christmas the most special one yet—not just for themselves, but for the entire town. They decided to hold a town-wide Christmas feast, open to anyone and everyone. Those who had extra would share, and those who had little would come and enjoy the warmth of community. The empty lot at the center of Maple

Street, which had been desolate for so long, would be transformed into a space for celebration, filled with tables, lights, and decorations.

As the townspeople dispersed, they didn't just leave with the idea of the feast—they left with a sense of purpose. Each person was determined to contribute something, no matter how small. Maple Street was coming alive again, and it wasn't because of the gifts the old man had given them, but because of the gift they had rediscovered within themselves: the gift of community.

The old man's letter was tucked away, but its message lingered in every heart. The true Christmas miracle was already happening, and soon the town would come together to witness it in full.

THE AIR ON MAPLE STREET was electric with anticipation as Christmas Eve approached. Every home was bustling with preparations, but it wasn't the frantic rush that had marked holidays in years past. This time, it was different. There was no competition over who had the brightest lights or the tallest tree. Instead, the focus was on coming together as a community, and every household had something to contribute to the grand Christmas Eve feast.

The vacant lot at the center of town, once bleak and lifeless, was now a festive wonderland. Children strung homemade paper chains between the lampposts, while the adults set up long tables covered in crisp white cloths. The town's few remaining shopkeepers had donated what they could—a mix of food, decorations, and supplies. The hardware store contributed extra lumber, which the men of the town used to construct a makeshift stage for carolers, and the bakery filled the air with the sweet scent of gingerbread and pies.

As dusk began to fall, lanterns and candles were lit, casting a soft glow over the snow-covered ground. The town square twinkled like a scene from a holiday card, with strings of lights winding around every tree, and a large Christmas tree now stood proudly in the middle of the square. But the most beautiful sight wasn't the decorations; it was the faces of the townspeople—smiling, laughing, and filled with a warmth that came not from the firepits they had set up, but from their rekindled sense of togetherness.

The spirit of the old man still lingered in their minds. Everyone remembered the mysterious gifts, and they whispered amongst themselves, wondering who he truly was. But there was little time to dwell on questions, as the town's first guests began to arrive—families from nearby villages who had heard of the feast and come to join in the celebration.

Then, as the final preparations were being made, a sudden hush fell over the crowd. At the edge of the square, standing just beyond the light of the lanterns, was the old man. His coat was still worn and ragged, and his boots were still dusted with snow, but there was something almost magical about him, as if the snow itself had brought him back to Maple Street. The townspeople turned to face him, their hearts pounding with a mixture of curiosity and wonder.

He walked slowly through the crowd, his eyes soft with kindness. People stepped aside, parting like the Red Sea, allowing him to move to the center of the square, right in front of the great Christmas tree. There, he reached into his coat and pulled out a letter, just like the one they had found on the bulletin board. With a nod of respect, he handed it to Mayor Grant.

Mayor Grant, his hands trembling slightly, opened the envelope and began to read aloud:

"To my dear friends on Maple Street,

I have watched you rediscover what truly matters, and now it is time for me to reveal the last gift I have for you—though it is not a gift of mine, but one you have already given each other.

You see, I am no stranger at all. You know me well, for I am the spirit of Christmas that you carry within your hearts. I come in many forms, sometimes as a humble old man, sometimes as a gentle snowfall, but always with the same purpose: to remind you of the power you hold to create miracles through love, kindness, and community.

Tonight, you have done just that. The miracle you have been waiting for has already happened—because you have made it so.

Let this feast be a reminder that no matter how hard times may get, you are never alone. As long as you have each other, there is always hope, always warmth, and always a reason to celebrate.

Merry Christmas to all of you. With all my love,

An old friend."

The mayor's voice wavered as he finished the letter, and by the time he folded the paper and tucked it back into the envelope, there wasn't a dry eye in the crowd. The townspeople looked at one another, realizing that the old man had been right all along. They had been waiting for a miracle, not realizing they had created it themselves through their kindness and love for one another.

It was then that the old man stepped forward, his eyes shining with the same warmth that had begun to fill their hearts. He smiled gently and raised his hand as if in farewell.

For a brief moment, he was bathed in the soft glow of the lanterns and Christmas lights, his figure standing tall amidst the snow. And then, just as suddenly as he had appeared, the old man turned and walked slowly down Maple Street, his footsteps fading into the night. By the time anyone thought to follow him, he was gone, leaving behind nothing but a trail of fresh snow and the echo of his message.

The townspeople stood in awe, the meaning of the old man's words sinking deep into their hearts. He wasn't just some stranger who had wandered into their lives; he was the embodiment of the Christmas spirit, reminding them that they held the power to create miracles. And tonight, they had done just that.

With renewed joy, the townspeople gathered around the tables, the feast about to begin. The sounds of laughter, song, and celebration filled the air, mixing with the gentle hum of Christmas carols that drifted through the crisp night.

This was a Christmas unlike any they had ever experienced—a Christmas not defined by what they had lost, but by what they had found in each other. Maple Street, once a place of quiet despair, now rang with the sounds of joy and hope, and the town's people knew that the miracle the old man had spoken of would live on long after the last candle had been blown out and the snow had melted.

Because miracles, they realized, were not just moments of magic—they were born from love, kindness, and the simple, powerful act of coming together. And that, more than anything, was the true gift of Christmas.

CHRISTMAS MORNING DAWNED crisp and bright on Maple Street. The snow that had blanketed the town in white still shimmered under the soft light of the rising sun, but now, it seemed less like a symbol of the hardships the town had faced and more like a fresh, clean beginning. The air was filled with the sound of children's laughter, and the smell of pine and cinnamon drifted from every home as families awoke to celebrate.

The town was transformed. Businesses that had been on the verge of closing suddenly saw a resurgence of customers—many of them being the same townspeople who had once lost hope. Neighbors who had once kept to themselves were now sharing coffee over fences, exchanging gifts of homemade jam and pies. And the children, who had spent months feeling the weight of their parents' struggles, were now out in the snow, building snowmen and exchanging stories of the night before.

The old, dark cloud of uncertainty that had hung over Maple Street had lifted. The town no longer looked at Christmas as just another day that passed, burdened with their troubles. Instead, it was a day that marked their rebirth as a community, a day filled with warmth, generosity, and the unmistakable glow of hope.

Mayor Grant stood in the town square that morning, the letter from the old man still tucked safely in his coat pocket. The town's Christmas tree sparkled behind him, its lights a reminder of the light that had returned to their hearts. He watched as people gathered in the square once again, but this time not to work or fix something broken—they gathered to enjoy each other's company, to be together.

Nearby, a small group of children played, their laughter carrying on the cold breeze. One of the children, a girl with bright eyes and a red scarf, noticed the mayor and ran over to him, tugging on his coat sleeve.

"Mayor Grant," she said with a big smile, "do you think he'll come back next Christmas?"

The mayor knelt down, looking into the girl's hopeful eyes. "Maybe he will," he said, "but even if he doesn't, we don't need to wait for him to bring another miracle. We can make our own."

The girl tilted her head, curious. "How?"

The mayor smiled warmly. "By being kind. By helping each other, like we did last night. The Christmas spirit is always with us, as long as we remember what it's really about."

The girl nodded thoughtfully and ran back to her friends, her scarf trailing behind her. Mayor Grant stood, watching as the children resumed their play, their laughter echoing through the square.

In the days and weeks that followed, the miracle of Maple Street spread far and wide. Word of the town's transformation and the mysterious old man reached neighboring towns, and soon people were coming from all over to witness the joy that had taken root there. Maple Street's shops reopened, businesses flourished, and the sense of togetherness that had been reignited on that magical Christmas Eve remained strong, even as winter gave way to spring.

But the people of Maple Street never forgot the old man. His gifts—small and simple—had sparked something within them that couldn't be extinguished. Every Christmas, they left a place for him at the feast, a reminder that miracles are not just the work of mysterious strangers, but of ordinary people who come together in love and kindness.

Years later, when the snow began to fall again and Christmas lights flickered to life on Maple Street, the townspeople gathered in the square as they always did. The children sang carols, and the adults exchanged smiles and stories of Christmases past. And while they no longer looked for the old man's return, they felt his presence in every act of kindness, in every shared meal, in every moment of warmth.

As they gathered for another Christmas feast, they knew that the true miracle wasn't something that had come from outside—it had come from within them, and it was a gift they would carry with them for all the Christmases to come.

The old man, whoever he was, had given them the greatest gift of all: the understanding that miracles happen when people believe in the power of love, community, and the spirit of Christmas.

And from that Christmas forward, Maple Street never faced hard times alone again.

The town had found its heart, and with it, the lasting joy of a Christmas miracle.

THAT CHRISTMAS EVE would forever be remembered as the night Maple Street came alive again. Every December, as the first snowflakes fell, the townspeople would gather and smile, knowing that miracles, no matter how small, were always possible on their beloved street.

And somewhere out there, maybe watching from a distance, the old man smiled, too.

The Gingerbread House Adventure

IT WAS CHRISTMAS EVE, and the air was filled with the smell of pine, cinnamon, and the faint scent of snow from the world outside. Inside, the cozy warmth of Sam and Lily's living room crackled with excitement. The fireplace glowed with soft orange flames, casting shadows that danced on the walls, while colorful Christmas lights twinkled on their tree, reflecting off shiny ornaments and ribbons.

Sam, the older of the two, was busy inspecting the gingerbread pieces laid out on the kitchen table. His brow furrowed in concentration, his tongue peeking out as he carefully fitted one wall of the gingerbread house to another. Lily, his younger sister, sat beside him, her small hands sticky with icing as she lined the roof with gumdrops, her eyes sparkling with delight.

"This is going to be the best gingerbread house ever," Sam said, stepping back to admire their work so far.

Lily nodded eagerly. "It has to be perfect. Santa might stop by to see it!"

Their parents had gone to bed early, leaving the siblings to finish their Christmas Eve tradition together. Every year, they built a gingerbread house—bigger, more detailed, and more ambitious than the last. This year, they had gone all out: candy cane pillars, chocolate bar doors, peppermint windows, and gumdrop bushes lining the front. It was a masterpiece.

With a soft hum of a Christmas carol, Lily added the final touch—a bright red gumdrop to the peak of the roof. “Done!” she exclaimed, clapping her hands together.

Sam grinned, wiping the icing from his hands on a dish towel. “It’s perfect.”

They both stood there for a moment, admiring their creation. The kitchen was bathed in a soft glow from the Christmas lights, making the gingerbread house look almost magical.

“I wish we could live in it,” Lily said dreamily.

Sam laughed. “Yeah, imagine that—a whole world made of candy. That would be—”

Suddenly, a soft sound interrupted his thoughts. It was faint, but unmistakable—a high-pitched voice, calling out. Sam and Lily exchanged a puzzled glance.

“Did you hear that?” Lily asked, her voice barely a whisper.

Before Sam could respond, the gingerbread house began to tremble. At first, it was just a tiny shiver, like the house itself was stretching, but then the front door of the house—made from a square of chocolate—swung open with a creak. Inside, two tiny gingerbread people stood at the threshold, waving frantically. Their icing faces looked worried, their gumdrop buttons shaking with each movement.

"Help us!" one of them cried out in a tiny, squeaky voice. "Our kingdom is in danger!"

Sam and Lily gasped in unison. The gingerbread people were alive!

SAM AND LILY STOOD frozen, their eyes wide as the two gingerbread people frantically waved at them from the doorway of the little house. It was impossible. Gingerbread wasn’t supposed to talk, much less move, but here they were, two tiny figures made of sugar and spice, calling for help.

"Did... did they just say 'help us'?" Lily whispered, clutching Sam's arm.

Sam nodded slowly, still staring in disbelief. "I think they did."

Before they could ask another question, the tiny gingerbread woman stepped forward, her icing eyes filled with worry. "Please, there isn't much time! The chocolate lava is coming! If we don't stop it, our entire kingdom will be flooded!"

"Chocolate lava?" Sam blinked. "What's going on?"

The gingerbread man hurried forward, his gumdrop buttons shaking with every step. "Yes! The chocolate river that flows through our kingdom has overflowed, and it's turning into a flood! If we don't stop it soon, it'll melt everything!"

Lily knelt down to get a better look at the tiny figures. "But how can we help?" she asked, her heart racing with excitement and concern.

The gingerbread woman looked up at her with hopeful eyes. "You built our home, so you must have the power to save it. You and your brother are the only ones who can help us."

Sam rubbed the back of his neck, still trying to process what was happening. "But... we're not gingerbread people. We're... well, we're human. How are we supposed to—"

Before he could finish, the ground beneath their feet gave a slight shake, and the air seemed to shimmer with a strange, sugary glow. The gingerbread people exchanged a knowing glance.

"It's happening," the gingerbread man said, turning to the siblings. "Hold on tight. You're about to shrink down to our size."

"What?" Sam gasped, but before he could move, a swirl of sparkling sugar dust began to surround him and Lily. They felt a strange tingling sensation as the room around them seemed to grow larger and larger—or, rather, they were getting smaller and smaller!

Within seconds, they were no taller than the gingerbread house itself.

"Whoa," Sam whispered, looking around in awe. Everything towered over them now—the kitchen table was a mountain, and the Christmas tree in the living room seemed like a forest. But most incredible of all was the gingerbread house, now transformed into a grand, candy-coated kingdom.

"We're... we're gingerbread size!" Lily exclaimed, spinning around and giggling as she examined her new perspective.

The gingerbread man smiled at them. "Welcome to our world, Sam and Lily. Now, come quickly! We must stop the chocolate lava before it's too late!"

Without hesitation, the siblings followed the gingerbread couple toward the house. As they stepped inside, they found themselves in a bustling, magical world made entirely of candy. The floors were polished sugar, the walls lined with licorice, and candy cane lampposts lit up the streets. Gingerbread people hurried around, looking anxious, their tiny hands carrying buckets of frosting and candy to reinforce the town's walls.

"Over there!" the gingerbread woman pointed toward the horizon, where a river of molten chocolate was flowing toward them, bubbling and steaming. The river was growing larger by the second, threatening to spill over its sugary banks and flood the entire kingdom.

Lily gasped. "What do we do? How do we stop it?"

The gingerbread man led them toward the edge of the kingdom. "We have to reach the Great Marshmallow Dam. It's the only thing that can stop the lava, but something's blocking the way!"

"What's blocking it?" Sam asked, already feeling the rush of adrenaline as the chocolate river surged closer.

The gingerbread woman's face grew grim. "The Toffee Monster. He's been terrorizing our kingdom for days, and now he's made things even worse. He's clogging the dam with his sticky toffee, and unless we defeat him, the chocolate lava will break through!"

Sam exchanged a determined glance with Lily. "Looks like we've got a mission."

Lily nodded, her eyes gleaming with excitement. "Let's go save the gingerbread kingdom!"

With the chocolate lava creeping closer, Sam and Lily took off toward the candy forest, ready to face whatever challenges awaited them. The adventure had just begun.

SAM AND LILY SPRINTED toward the candy forest, their footsteps light on the sugar-dusted path. As they entered the forest, towering lollipop trees and gumdrop bushes surrounded them, casting colorful shadows in the sweet sunlight. The path ahead twisted through licorice vines and candy cane trunks, but despite the beauty of the scene, there was a sense of urgency in the air.

The gingerbread man, who introduced himself as Captain Crumb, led the way, his small feet pattering against the candy ground. His wife, Mrs. Sugar, followed close behind, her icing dress fluttering in the breeze.

"We must be careful," Captain Crumb warned, glancing over his shoulder. "The candy forest can be tricky. There are dangerous traps, and the Toffee Monster's minions might be lurking."

Sam nodded. "We're ready for anything," he said bravely, though his heart raced in anticipation.

Lily looked around, wide-eyed with wonder. "This place is amazing," she whispered, but then her face turned serious. "But how do we stop the Toffee Monster?"

Mrs. Sugar smiled warmly at Lily. "With teamwork, of course. The two of you have already shown great courage by coming here. Together, we'll figure it out."

Just as she spoke, the ground beneath them suddenly shifted, and Lily let out a yelp as her foot sank into something soft and squishy. Sam grabbed her arm, pulling her back just in time.

"Careful!" he exclaimed. "It's marshmallow quicksand!"

Sure enough, beneath them was a patch of gooey white marshmallow, slowly pulling them in. Captain Crumb and Mrs. Sugar scrambled to the side, just out of reach of the sticky trap.

"We'll have to find another way around!" Captain Crumb said, surveying the marshmallow pit.

Sam scanned the surroundings, thinking quickly. "Look! We can use those licorice vines," he said, pointing to a thick bunch of red vines hanging from a nearby candy cane tree.

Lily's eyes lit up. "Great idea!" She grabbed one end of the licorice and tied it to a branch, while Sam did the same on the other side.

"Everyone hold on tight," Sam instructed. One by one, they carefully swung across the marshmallow quicksand, the licorice creaking but holding firm under their weight. Sam was the last to cross, landing safely on the other side with a proud grin.

"That was close," Lily breathed, her heart pounding. "What's next?"

As they continued deeper into the forest, the sounds of the chocolate lava growing closer reached their ears, a constant reminder of the ticking clock. But soon, another sound joined it—a low, rumbling growl that echoed through the trees.

"What's that?" Lily whispered, eyes wide.

From behind a large gumdrop bush, a hulking shadow emerged. It was the Toffee Monster. He towered over them, made entirely of thick, sticky toffee. His arms were long and dripped with caramel, and his eyes glowed with a molten brown hue. He let out a roar that sent shivers down Sam and Lily's spines.

"So, you've come to stop me?" the Toffee Monster growled, his voice thick and syrupy. "You'll never make it to the dam. This kingdom will be drowned in chocolate, and then it will be mine to rule!"

Sam stepped forward, fists clenched. "We won't let that happen!"

The Toffee Monster laughed, a deep, bubbling sound. "Oh really? Let's see if you can get past me!"

With that, he swung one of his caramel arms toward them, sending a wave of sticky toffee in their direction. Sam and Lily ducked just in time, but the toffee splattered against the ground, trapping Captain Crumb and Mrs. Sugar.

"Help!" Mrs. Sugar cried, struggling to free herself from the gooey mess.

Lily's mind raced. "Sam, we need to distract him!"

Sam nodded, thinking quickly. "I've got an idea. Lily, see that pile of sprinkles over there?" He pointed to a colorful mound near a candy rock. "Maybe we can use it to blind him."

Lily grinned, catching on. "On it!"

As the Toffee Monster prepared to attack again, Lily darted toward the sprinkles. Sam grabbed a nearby candy cane and waved it in the monster's face, taunting him. "Hey, over here! You're too slow!" he shouted.

The Toffee Monster roared in frustration and lunged at Sam, his toffee arms flailing. But just as he swung, Lily tossed a handful of sprinkles right into his eyes.

"Argh!" the Toffee Monster bellowed, stumbling back as the sprinkles stuck to his sticky face. "I can't see!"

With the monster distracted, Sam rushed over to Captain Crumb and Mrs. Sugar, using his candy cane to cut through the toffee that trapped them. "Quick, let's get to the dam while he's blinded!"

The group sprinted away as the Toffee Monster continued to stumble around, trying to clear the sprinkles from his face. The sound of rushing chocolate lava grew louder as they neared the Great Marshmallow Dam.

But when they arrived, Sam and Lily gasped. The dam was clogged with thick toffee, blocking it from holding back the lava. In the distance, the molten chocolate bubbled and surged, inching closer and closer to the kingdom.

“There it is,” Captain Crumb said breathlessly. “If we can clear the toffee, we can stop the flood!”

Lily turned to Sam, determination shining in her eyes. “We’ve come this far. Let’s finish what we started.”

With time running out, Sam and Lily grabbed candy tools and began chipping away at the toffee, knowing that the fate of the gingerbread kingdom rested in their hands.

SAM AND LILY WORKED frantically, chipping away at the sticky toffee that clogged the Great Marshmallow Dam. The thick goo was harder to remove than they expected, clinging stubbornly to the dam’s surface as the chocolate lava surged ever closer.

"Faster, Lily!" Sam urged, his hands trembling from the effort.

"I’m trying!" Lily replied, using her candy cane pick to scrape off large chunks of toffee. “This stuff is like glue!”

Captain Crumb and Mrs. Sugar joined in, their small hands working alongside the siblings, but the lava kept inching closer, a bubbling river of molten chocolate threatening to engulf the candy kingdom.

“We’re running out of time!” Mrs. Sugar cried, her voice high with panic.

Sam glanced at the approaching flood, his mind racing. "Wait a minute!" he said suddenly, his eyes lighting up with an idea. "The chocolate lava is hot, right? What if we melt the toffee with it?"

Lily stopped scraping and stared at him. "Melt it with the lava? But how do we control it?"

Captain Crumb's face brightened with realization. "The peppermint pipes!" he exclaimed. "They run through the dam to release small amounts of water or chocolate to maintain balance. We could use them to direct a bit of the lava toward the toffee and melt it!"

Sam's heart raced with excitement. "That's it! If we open the peppermint pipes, we can guide just enough lava to melt the toffee and clear the dam."

Lily nodded, determined. "It's risky, but it's our only chance."

They rushed toward the peppermint valve at the base of the dam, a large wheel made of striped candy. With Captain Crumb's help, Sam and Lily began to turn it. At first, the wheel resisted, but with a few more twists, it creaked and started to turn.

"Careful," Sam warned. "We only need a little bit of lava."

The valve hissed, and the ground trembled as a thin stream of chocolate lava diverted from the river and began flowing through the peppermint pipes. It snaked its way toward the dam, glowing with molten heat. Sam held his breath as the lava made contact with the hardened toffee.

"It's working!" Lily cheered as the toffee began to bubble and melt, turning soft under the intense heat.

The lava slowly dissolved the toffee, clearing a path for the dam to function again. With the blockage gone, the marshmallow dam flexed and released a gush of cooling marshmallow cream into the lava river, stopping the molten flow in its tracks.

The chocolate lava began to cool and solidify, hardening into a smooth chocolate surface. The flood was stopped, and the gingerbread kingdom was saved.

"We did it!" Sam shouted, jumping in excitement.

Captain Crumb clapped his sugary hands together. "You've saved us! The kingdom is safe!"

Lily let out a breath of relief, wiping her sticky hands on her shirt. "I can't believe we actually did it."

Mrs. Sugar beamed at the siblings, her eyes sparkling with gratitude. "You two are true heroes. The kingdom owes you everything."

The ground gave another small tremor, but this time it wasn't a warning. Instead, the sugary glow from before returned, surrounding Sam and Lily in a sparkling swirl of frosting and magic.

"What's happening now?" Sam asked, his voice tinged with awe.

Captain Crumb smiled warmly. "It's time for you to return home. You've done what you came here to do."

The glow intensified, and Sam and Lily felt the world around them begin to shift. The candy trees, the marshmallow dam, and the gingerbread people all blurred into a whirlwind of colors as the magic carried them away.

The last thing they saw was Captain Crumb and Mrs. Sugar waving goodbye, their gingerbread faces full of joy and gratitude.

"Goodbye!" Lily called out, her voice echoing as they were lifted up and away, back to the world they came from.

SAM AND LILY BLINKED their eyes open, feeling the warmth of the fireplace beside them and the cozy softness of their living room carpet beneath their feet. The gingerbread kingdom was gone, and they were back in their home. Outside, the snow fell gently, covering the world in a blanket of white, but inside, everything was peaceful.

Lily sat up, rubbing her eyes. "Did... did that really happen?"

Sam looked around, trying to process what they had just experienced. The gingerbread house sat on the table in front of them, exactly as they had left it the night before. But something was different. A soft, magical glow shimmered faintly around the edges of the house, like the sparkle of snow on a winter morning.

"I think it did," Sam said with a smile, pointing at the gingerbread house. "Look."

Lily gasped as she noticed the same glow. She reached out to touch it but stopped, almost not wanting to disturb the magic. "It's beautiful," she whispered. "I guess we really did help the gingerbread people."

Sam nodded, feeling a sense of pride and warmth. "We saved their kingdom, and now everything's back to normal."

As they sat there, the smell of freshly baked cookies and cinnamon filled the air, and the Christmas tree lights twinkled brightly in the corner. It was Christmas morning, but somehow, it felt more magical than any Christmas they had ever experienced before.

Just then, their parents entered the room, smiling warmly at their children.

"Merry Christmas!" their mom said, carrying a tray of hot cocoa. "You two were up late last night. I hope you got some rest."

Sam and Lily exchanged a knowing look but said nothing about their gingerbread adventure. Some things were too special to explain.

"We did," Sam replied with a grin. "It was the best Christmas Eve ever."

Their dad glanced at the gingerbread house and raised an eyebrow. "That's quite the gingerbread house you built! It almost looks like it's glowing."

Lily and Sam shared another smile. "Yeah, it turned out better than we expected," Lily said, winking at Sam.

The family gathered around the Christmas tree, opening gifts and laughing together as the morning passed. But every so often, Sam and Lily would steal a glance at the gingerbread house, its glow still faintly twinkling as if to remind them of the incredible adventure they had shared.

As the day went on, snow continued to fall outside, blanketing the world in silence. Sam and Lily felt a sense of calm and joy, knowing that they had been part of something truly magical. They had ventured into a world of candy, faced danger, and saved a kingdom, all in one unforgettable Christmas Eve.

And as they sipped their hot cocoa by the fire, Sam turned to Lily and whispered, “Do you think we'll ever go back?”

Lily smiled, her eyes sparkling with wonder. “Maybe. But even if we don't, I'll never forget what we did. We're heroes, Sam.”

Sam grinned, feeling the warmth of the Christmas magic all around him. “Yeah. We're heroes.”

And with that, they settled into the cozy embrace of the holiday, knowing that Christmas would always hold a special place in their hearts—because somewhere, in a sweet, magical kingdom, a gingerbread house was glowing just a little brighter, thanks to them.

The Snowman Who Stole Christmas

IT WAS THE DAY BEFORE Christmas, and the small town of Pine Hollow was buzzing with excitement. Twinkling lights draped over every rooftop, wreaths adorned each door, and the scent of pine trees and freshly baked gingerbread filled the air. Children ran through the streets, their laughter echoing as they tossed snowballs and made snow angels. Everywhere you looked, there was joy, warmth, and holiday cheer.

At the heart of all this excitement was Lucy, a curious and kind-hearted girl of eight, with bright eyes and a contagious smile. Lucy loved Christmas more than anyone. To her, it wasn't just about the presents or the delicious food—it was about the magic that filled the air, the way the whole town came together to celebrate. Every year, she helped her parents decorate their little house on the hill, carefully placing each ornament on the tree and singing along to her favorite carols.

This year, though, Lucy felt an extra tingle of excitement. There was more snow than usual, and something in the air felt... different, like the kind of magic she always dreamed of might actually come to life.

And she wasn't wrong.

Just outside of town, in a quiet field blanketed by snow, stood Frosty. He was an ordinary snowman—or at least, he had been. Carved out of fresh snow with button eyes, a carrot nose, and a scarf too big for his round, icy frame, he stood still, watching the town from a distance.

Frosty had been built by a few neighborhood kids earlier that week, and though they had laughed and played while shaping him, they had quickly forgotten about him as soon as they went back home to the warmth of their firesides.

Frosty, however, had not forgotten.

As the stars began to twinkle in the sky on Christmas Eve, something extraordinary happened. The soft glow of the moon seemed to sparkle in the snow, and a gentle breeze swirled around the lonely snowman. A single snowflake, larger than the rest, landed on his nose, and at that moment, something magical stirred inside him.

His button eyes blinked. His twig arms wiggled. Frosty the Snowman had come to life!

At first, he was amazed. He looked around, moving his snowy limbs in wonder. He could walk! He could move! But as his excitement began to settle, Frosty felt something else—a pang of sadness. He looked at the town, bustling with happiness, and realized he had no place in it. No family to share gifts with, no warm house to call home. Everyone was inside, wrapped in love and warmth, while he stood alone in the cold.

Bitterness grew in his icy heart. He had been forgotten, and now, as he watched the lights twinkle in the distance, an idea formed in his mind. If he couldn't be part of the celebration, then maybe he could take away what made Christmas special to the townspeople—their decorations, their joy.

With a mischievous grin, Frosty began to march toward the town, determined to steal Christmas.

AS NIGHT FELL OVER Pine Hollow, the town glistened in its festive glory. String lights twinkled in every tree, and garlands hung from the lampposts. Houses were lined with glowing reindeer, snowflake ornaments, and shimmering wreaths. From his hiding spot in the shadows, Frosty watched it all with a bitter gleam in his eyes.

"Why should they have all the fun?" he muttered to himself, his twig fingers curling into fists. "If I can't be part of Christmas, neither can they."

With a determined stomp of his snowy foot, Frosty crept into the nearest yard. It belonged to the baker, Mrs. Whittaker, whose house was famously adorned with more decorations than anyone else in town. The yard was a winter wonderland—candy cane lights bordered the walkway, a glowing Santa waved from the porch, and an enormous star lit up the roof. Frosty eyed the decorations with a mischievous grin.

One by one, he began to steal them. First, he plucked the candy cane lights out of the ground and shoved them under his arm. Then, he pulled down the star from the roof and stuffed it into the scarf wrapped around his neck. With a gleeful chuckle, he waddled over to Santa, grabbed him by his glowing beard, and tossed him into a pile of snow. By the time he was done, Mrs. Whittaker's house looked plain and bare, as if Christmas had skipped right over it.

Frosty moved on to the next house, and then the next. At each one, he swiped lights, ornaments, and anything that glittered or glowed. Slowly but surely, he turned the once-festive town into a gloomy, decoration-free zone. The lights on the main street were the first to go, followed by the giant Christmas tree in the town square. Frosty left nothing behind but darkness and confusion.

By morning, Pine Hollow was in disarray. The townspeople awoke to find their Christmas cheer had been stolen. "Where are all the decorations?" someone cried. "Who would do such a thing?" another shouted, bewildered.

Lucy, who had been eagerly waiting to help her parents finish decorating their own house, looked out the window and gasped. The twinkling lights that had filled the streets were gone. The wreaths and ornaments vanished. Even the star on top of the town's Christmas tree was missing.

She hurried outside, running from house to house, trying to understand what had happened. As she reached the town square, she overheard her neighbors talking in confusion.

"It's like someone's trying to ruin Christmas," Mr. Jenkins, the postman, said with a frown.

"They've taken everything!" Mrs. Whittaker added, shaking her head in disbelief.

Lucy's heart sank. Who would want to steal Christmas?

As she turned to go back home, something caught her eye in the distance. A figure—round and waddling—was disappearing into the woods, a string of lights trailing from his snowy hands. Lucy squinted and gasped.

"It's the snowman!" she whispered, eyes wide.

Without a second thought, Lucy ran toward the woods, determined to find out why Frosty was stealing Christmas. She was scared, but her curiosity and kindness pushed her forward. Whoever this snowman was, she was sure there had to be a reason for his mischief.

As she followed his tracks in the snow, Lucy's heart pounded with anticipation. Little did she know that her life—and Frosty's—was about to change forever.

LUCY CAREFULLY FOLLOWED the trail of scattered lights and tinsel into the woods. The further she went, the quieter it became, the festive sounds of the town fading into the distance. Her boots crunched in the snow as she pushed through the frosty trees, determined to catch up to the mischievous snowman.

Finally, she spotted him.

Frosty stood in a small clearing, arms loaded with stolen decorations, his icy face twisted in a frown. Around him lay a messy pile of Christmas lights, ornaments, and tattered wreaths, all hastily tossed into a heap. Lucy watched from behind a tree for a moment, her breath forming small clouds in the cold air. She had expected to find a villain, but instead, she saw something different. Frosty didn't look angry or menacing—he looked... sad.

Gathering her courage, Lucy stepped forward. "Hey!" she called out, her voice small but steady.

Frosty jumped and spun around, his button eyes widening in surprise. "Who—who are you?" he stammered, taking a step back, clearly not expecting to be discovered.

"I'm Lucy," she said, walking closer, her heart pounding. "I saw you... stealing the decorations. But why? Why would you want to ruin Christmas?"

For a moment, Frosty didn't answer. He looked down at the snow, kicking a loose ornament with his twig foot. "I didn't want to ruin Christmas," he muttered, his voice barely above a whisper. "I just... I just didn't want to be left out."

Lucy blinked. "Left out? But... you're a snowman! You're a part of Christmas already. People love snowmen."

Frosty shook his head. "Not me. They built me and then forgot all about me. No one invited me to their parties or put me by their warm fires. I'm just out here in the cold, alone." His voice cracked a little, and Lucy could hear the loneliness behind his words.

For a moment, she was quiet, thinking about how Frosty must have felt, watching all the joy from the outside. She couldn't imagine what it would be like to feel so isolated during the happiest time of year. Then, her face softened with understanding.

"I'm sorry, Frosty," she said, stepping even closer. "That must feel awful. But stealing all the decorations won't make things better.

Christmas isn't about lights or ornaments. It's about being together, with family and friends. It's about love."

Frosty's eyes flickered with confusion. "Love? But how can I be part of that? I'm just a snowman."

Lucy smiled warmly. "You don't have to be anything special to be part of Christmas. You just have to be with people who care about you. Come with me—I'll show you."

Frosty hesitated, glancing back at the pile of stolen decorations. "But... what if they don't want me? What if they're angry because I took everything?"

"They might be upset at first," Lucy admitted, "but if you show them you're sorry and help fix things, they'll forgive you. They'll understand."

Frosty was quiet for a long moment, staring down at his twig hands. Then, with a deep breath, he nodded. "Okay. I'll try."

Lucy's face lit up with a bright smile. "Come on, let's go. I'll help you return everything."

Together, they gathered up the decorations, untangling lights and picking up ornaments. As they worked, Lucy talked to Frosty about the town, about all the families and the way they celebrated Christmas. She told him stories about caroling in the snow, drinking hot cocoa by the fire, and how everyone came together to light the giant tree in the town square.

Frosty listened, his icy heart slowly melting with each word. For the first time, he didn't feel so alone. Lucy's kindness and friendship wrapped around him like the warmth he had always longed for.

By the time they were ready to return to the town, Frosty felt different—lighter, happier. He was still nervous, but with Lucy by his side, he knew he could make things right.

Together, they set off back to Pine Hollow, ready to restore the Christmas spirit Frosty had nearly stolen.

LUCY AND FROSTY APPROACHED the edge of Pine Hollow, their arms full of stolen decorations. The town was eerily quiet, its once-cheerful streets now bare and dark. Houses that had glowed with Christmas lights the night before were now shadowed, their yards stripped of festive cheer. Frosty's stomach—or what felt like one—churned with guilt.

"They're going to hate me," Frosty muttered, glancing at Lucy.

Lucy shook her head with a kind smile. "They won't hate you, Frosty. We'll make things right together. You'll see."

Still uncertain but trusting Lucy, Frosty followed her into the town square. As they arrived, the townspeople began to gather, curious about the noise and movement. At first, there were murmurs of confusion—then, gasps of recognition.

"There's the snowman!" someone shouted.

"Is that where all our decorations went?" another voice called out.

Frosty froze, the string of lights he was holding slipping from his snowy hands. He could see the looks of anger and frustration on people's faces. His twig arms shook with fear, but before he could turn to flee, Lucy stepped forward.

"Wait!" she called out to the crowd, her voice ringing out strong and clear. "It's not what you think. Frosty didn't mean to ruin Christmas—he was just lonely. He didn't understand what Christmas was really about."

The crowd fell silent, all eyes on Lucy as she continued. "He thought Christmas was just decorations and lights, but I told him it's about being together. About friendship and love. Frosty wants to make things right—he's here to help return everything he took."

There was a pause, and then a voice from the crowd spoke up. It was Mrs. Whittaker, the baker. "Is that true, Frosty?" she asked, her tone softening. "Were you just lonely?"

Frosty shuffled forward, looking down at his twig feet. "I... I didn't mean to hurt anyone," he said, his voice barely a whisper. "I just felt like I didn't belong. I thought if I took the decorations, maybe people would notice me. But I see now that I was wrong. Christmas isn't about things—it's about people. I'm really sorry."

There was a murmur through the crowd. People exchanged glances, and slowly, the hard lines of their faces softened. The spirit of Christmas was about forgiveness, after all. And seeing the snowman standing there, so remorseful and sad, they couldn't stay angry.

"Well," Mrs. Whittaker said after a moment, "Christmas is about second chances too. Let's help him put everything back!"

One by one, the townspeople stepped forward, offering their hands to Frosty and Lucy. Together, they began to work, stringing lights back onto houses, hanging ornaments, and restoring the festive cheer that had been stolen. Lucy and Frosty worked side by side, and soon, the town was once again sparkling with Christmas magic.

Frosty smiled as he tied a bow onto a wreath and hung it on the town hall door. For the first time in his short life, he felt truly part of something. The warmth of the community surrounded him, even though he was made of snow.

As the final touch, Lucy handed Frosty the star that had once topped the giant Christmas tree in the town square. "You should do the honors," she said with a grin.

Frosty beamed and carefully placed the glowing star back on top of the tree. As soon as it was in place, the tree lit up in all its glory, casting a soft, golden light over the entire square. The crowd erupted into cheers, their Christmas spirit fully restored.

Tears of joy sparkled in Lucy's eyes as she looked at Frosty. "See?" she said. "I told you they'd forgive you."

Frosty nodded, overwhelmed with gratitude. "I don't know what I would've done without you, Lucy."

The townspeople gathered around the tree, singing carols and sharing laughter, and Frosty stood among them, no longer feeling like an outsider. He had found his place. He was no longer just a lonely snowman; he was part of Pine Hollow's Christmas.

With Lucy by his side, Frosty learned that Christmas wasn't about what you could take—it was about what you could give. And in giving back the joy he had taken, he had found the true meaning of the holiday.

As the snow fell softly around them, Lucy and Frosty joined the townspeople in celebrating a Christmas they would never forget.

THE MORNING OF CHRISTMAS dawned over Pine Hollow, casting a soft pink and golden light over the snow-covered town. The square, which had been filled with chaos and confusion the night before, now glowed with warmth and joy. The decorations were back in place, the tree stood tall and gleaming, and the air was filled with the sound of laughter and carols.

At the center of it all stood Frosty, no longer a lonely figure on the outskirts, but surrounded by the people of Pine Hollow. Children giggled and ran circles around him, tossing snowballs and tugging at his scarf, while the adults smiled and exchanged gifts. Frosty, once cold and distant, now felt a warmth in his heart that no amount of snow could freeze.

Lucy stood beside him, watching the scene unfold with a happy glow on her face. "See, Frosty?" she said. "You're part of Christmas now. You belong here."

Frosty nodded, his button eyes glimmering with gratitude. "I've never felt like this before," he admitted. "I always thought I didn't matter, but now... I realize it's not about being perfect. It's about being with people who care."

"And we care about you," Lucy said, smiling up at him. "You're one of us now. Pine Hollow wouldn't be the same without you."

Just then, Mrs. Whittaker approached, carrying a steaming mug of hot cocoa. "Here you go, Frosty," she said, handing it to him with a wink. "I know you can't drink it, but it's the thought that counts, right?"

Frosty chuckled, carefully holding the mug in his twig hands. "It's perfect," he said, touched by the gesture.

As the day went on, the townspeople included Frosty in every Christmas tradition. They sang carols around the tree, shared holiday stories, and even built more snowmen to keep Frosty company. For the first time in his life, Frosty wasn't just a decoration in the background—he was part of the heart and soul of Pine Hollow's Christmas.

That evening, as the sun set and the first stars began to twinkle in the sky, the townspeople gathered around the tree for one final tradition. Lucy stood beside Frosty, her eyes shining with excitement.

"Every year," she explained, "we make a special Christmas wish. Something from the heart. It doesn't have to be big—just something you hope for."

Frosty looked down at Lucy, then out at the crowd of smiling faces around him. He had already received more than he could have ever wished for. But there was one thing he still hoped for.

"I wish," Frosty began, his voice soft, "that Christmas could always be like this. That no one would ever feel left out or forgotten. I wish everyone could feel the warmth and love that I've felt today."

Lucy smiled and squeezed his twig hand. "That's a wonderful wish, Frosty."

As the townspeople made their own wishes and the stars above twinkled brighter, Frosty felt a deep sense of peace. He had learned the true meaning of Christmas—not in the decorations or gifts, but in the simple acts of kindness, love, and friendship. He had found his place, not just in Pine Hollow, but in the hearts of the people who had accepted him as one of their own.

And as the snow fell gently around them, Frosty knew that this Christmas, and every Christmas after, would be full of warmth, joy, and the spirit of togetherness.

Because now, Frosty wasn't just a snowman—he was a part of Pine Hollow's Christmas tradition, and the town wouldn't be the same without him.

As the final carol of the night echoed through the snowy streets, Frosty stood tall, his heart full, and his spirit forever warmed by the love and friendship he had found.

And so, Pine Hollow celebrated Christmas with renewed joy, knowing that even a mischievous snowman could find his place in their community—and in their hearts.

A Midnight Sleigh Ride

THE HOUSE WAS QUIET, save for the soft ticking of the clock on the mantel. A faint glow from the fireplace cast long, flickering shadows on the walls of the living room. Henry sat in his worn armchair, staring at the flames as if they held the answers to the sadness lodged deep in his heart. Across the room, Charlie was perched on the windowsill, his small frame hunched as he peered out at the snow falling softly outside. The silence between them had grown, filling the space where laughter and warmth once thrived.

It was Christmas Eve, but the usual excitement of the holiday seemed distant, almost foreign. The tree stood in the corner, half-decorated, its ornaments reflecting the dim light with a dull gleam. Presents were piled underneath, but there were fewer this year—each gift chosen out of obligation rather than joy.

Henry's heart still ached from the loss of his wife, Sarah. It had been a year since she passed, but the wound felt fresh, the emptiness ever present. Christmas had been her favorite time of year. She would fill the house with the smell of cinnamon and pine, humming festive tunes while she baked treats or strung lights around the tree. Now, without her, Henry could hardly bear the thought of celebrating. Every wreath, every carol, felt like a painful reminder of what he had lost.

Charlie, barely eight years old, sat quietly by the window, his breath fogging up the glass as he watched the world outside. He didn't ask for much this year. In fact, he hadn't asked for anything at all. His letters to

Santa had stopped, and the gleam in his eyes had faded, replaced by a sadness too heavy for someone his age to carry.

Henry glanced at him, guilt creeping in. He knew Charlie missed his mother deeply, but he didn't know how to bridge the gap that had grown between them. It was like they were both trapped in their own grief, unable to reach out to one another. Henry sighed and looked down at his hands, rough and calloused, feeling as if he had failed his son in more ways than one.

"Charlie," Henry said softly, his voice hoarse, "you should go to bed soon. It's getting late."

Charlie didn't respond at first, his eyes still fixed on the snowy landscape beyond the window. Then, after a long pause, he whispered, "Do you think Mom would have liked the tree?"

Henry felt a lump form in his throat. He hadn't expected the question, and for a moment, he didn't know what to say. The truth was, the tree looked nothing like the ones Sarah used to decorate—those trees had been full of life, color, and joy. This one felt empty, like it was missing the heart of Christmas.

"Yeah," Henry managed, his voice barely audible. "She would have loved it."

Charlie nodded slightly but said nothing more, his gaze distant as the snow continued to fall. The silence between them stretched on, heavy with unspoken words. Henry leaned back in his chair, closing his eyes for a moment, wondering how he would ever make things right.

THE CLOCK STRUCK MIDNIGHT, its chimes echoing faintly through the quiet house. Henry stirred from his chair, the warmth of the fire starting to fade as the embers dimmed. He glanced at Charlie, who remained by the window, unmoving. The snow outside had thickened, blanketing the world in a soft, white glow.

Suddenly, Charlie gasped, his small hands pressing against the window. "Dad! Look!"

Henry turned, his brow furrowing. "What is it, Charlie?"

"A reindeer! There's a reindeer in our yard!" Charlie's voice was filled with a rare spark of excitement, something Henry hadn't heard in months.

Henry frowned, rising slowly from his chair and walking over to the window. Sure enough, there, standing in the middle of their snow-covered yard, was a magnificent reindeer. Its fur shimmered in the moonlight, and its large, dark eyes seemed to twinkle as if filled with some ancient magic. But what caught Henry's attention most was the sleigh attached to it—a beautiful, ornate sleigh, trimmed with gold and silver, its polished wood gleaming against the snow.

"That can't be real," Henry muttered, rubbing his eyes in disbelief. "Reindeer don't just... show up like that."

Charlie's face was pressed against the glass, his breath fogging up the window again. "Dad, it's real! Look at the sleigh! Can we go? Please?"

Henry hesitated. The sensible part of him wanted to dismiss the whole thing as some odd illusion, but another part—one that had been buried under layers of grief—felt a flicker of curiosity. The reindeer stood motionless, watching them patiently, as if waiting for something.

Then, as if on cue, the reindeer lowered its head and shook the sleigh bells hanging from its antlers, the sound filling the air with a cheerful jingle. The sleigh, seemingly enchanted, slid forward slightly, its reins loose, inviting them to climb aboard.

Charlie's eyes were wide with wonder. "Please, Dad? Just this once?"

Henry looked down at his son, seeing the excitement in his eyes—the kind of excitement he hadn't seen in far too long. It was the first time Charlie had asked for something since Sarah had passed. How could he say no?

"Alright," Henry said quietly, still unsure if this was a dream or reality. "Let's see where this goes."

Charlie practically leaped from the windowsill, throwing on his coat and boots in a frenzy. Henry followed, grabbing his jacket and hat, his heart racing as they stepped out into the cold night. The snow crunched beneath their feet as they approached the reindeer, who bowed its head slightly in acknowledgment. The sleigh looked even more magical up close, its craftsmanship flawless, as if it had been plucked straight from the pages of a fairy tale.

"Go ahead," Henry said, motioning for Charlie to climb in first.

Charlie eagerly clambered into the sleigh, his eyes wide with anticipation. Henry hesitated for a moment, glancing at the reindeer, which met his gaze with a knowing look. He shook his head, still struggling to believe any of this was happening, but then he climbed in beside Charlie, wrapping his arm around his son to keep him warm.

As soon as Henry settled into the seat, the reindeer let out a soft snort and raised its head to the sky. With a sudden burst of energy, it leaped forward, pulling the sleigh with ease as they soared into the night. The snow-covered yard disappeared beneath them, and in seconds, they were gliding through the sky, the stars twinkling above and the world spread out below in a blanket of white.

Henry tightened his grip on Charlie, who was grinning ear to ear, his face lit up with pure joy. The wind whipped past them, but the cold didn't bite—instead, it felt refreshing, almost exhilarating. Henry's heart raced, a strange sense of wonder and peace washing over him for the first time in what felt like forever.

"Where are we going?" Charlie asked, his voice filled with awe.

Henry glanced around, unsure. "I don't know, buddy. But I guess we'll find out soon enough."

As they flew higher, the reindeer guided them through the vast, snowy expanse, weaving through clouds and over twinkling towns below. The stars seemed to glow brighter, as if lighting the way for their magical journey.

And in that moment, for the first time in a long while, Henry felt something stir deep inside him—a glimmer of the Christmas spirit he thought had been lost forever.

THE SLEIGH SOARED THROUGH the crisp night air, each moment feeling more surreal than the last. The snowy countryside stretched far beneath them, but it wasn't long before the landscape began to change. Ahead, shimmering lights danced on the horizon, and soon Henry and Charlie found themselves approaching the first of several magical destinations.

The sleigh descended gently, landing in front of a grand, gleaming ice castle. Its towering spires sparkled under the moonlight, each structure carved with intricate patterns that looked as if they had been formed by the hands of a master artisan. The walls glowed with a faint blue light, and as they approached, the heavy doors creaked open, welcoming them inside.

Charlie gasped in awe, his breath fogging the air. "Dad, look! It's like something from a storybook."

Henry nodded, his eyes widening as they stepped inside the castle. The interior was just as magical—massive ice sculptures of reindeer, snowflakes, and swirling patterns lined the hallways. Icicles hung from vaulted ceilings like glittering chandeliers. But despite the cold structure, the air inside was warm, almost comforting, as if the castle was enchanted to protect them from the winter chill.

As they wandered through the halls, Charlie couldn't stop grinning, running ahead to explore the sculptures and carvings. Henry followed slowly, his heart lightening with each step. The sadness that had gripped him so tightly for months began to ease as he watched

Charlie's joy bloom once again. It was as if this place, this journey, was waking something inside both of them.

After some time, the reindeer appeared again at the castle entrance, stamping its hoof softly as if signaling their time to move on. Henry placed a hand on Charlie's shoulder, smiling for what felt like the first time in ages.

"Come on, let's see what's next."

Back in the sleigh, they took off once more, the cold wind now refreshing instead of biting. As they flew through the night, the next destination came into view: a bustling village of toy-making elves. Bright lights twinkled in every window, and the sound of tiny hammers, laughter, and music echoed through the air as they touched down in the center of the village.

Elves, no taller than Charlie, were everywhere—dressed in bright green and red, each one busily working on toys of all shapes and sizes. Wooden trains, stuffed animals, dolls, and other whimsical creations lined the streets. One elf, with a mischievous grin and a twinkle in his eye, waved them over.

"Welcome, welcome!" the elf chirped. "Would you care to try your hand at making a Christmas toy?"

Charlie's face lit up. "Can we, Dad?"

Henry chuckled, nodding. "Why not?"

They spent the next few minutes at a workbench, Charlie trying his hand at assembling a wooden airplane while Henry marveled at the craftsmanship of the elves around him. Laughter filled the air, and for the first time in months, Henry felt himself truly relax. The weight of his grief began to lift as he watched Charlie focus on his toy, his son's smile a sight he hadn't seen in so long.

As the village's clock tower chimed softly, signaling the approach of midnight, the reindeer appeared once more, its bells jingling lightly. Henry knew it was time to continue their journey.

"Come on, Charlie. Let's see where this sleigh takes us next."

With a quick farewell to the elves, they climbed back into the sleigh and set off again. The night sky above them glittered with stars, and soon, they began their descent toward their final stop: a beautiful frozen lake.

The lake stretched out in front of them like a sheet of glass, reflecting the starry sky above. It was peaceful, serene, and utterly breathtaking. The sleigh landed gently on the shore, and the reindeer shook its bells, nodding toward the frozen surface as if encouraging them to step out.

Charlie's eyes widened in amazement. "It's like a mirror, Dad."

Henry smiled softly. "It really is."

They stepped onto the ice, hand in hand, and to their surprise, the surface wasn't slippery at all—it was firm, steady, and cool beneath their feet. They began to walk, the sound of their footsteps echoing faintly in the quiet night. As they wandered across the lake, something magical began to happen. Above them, the stars shimmered, and tiny flurries of snow fell gently, but it wasn't cold—it felt almost like a gentle caress, wrapping them in warmth and comfort.

Charlie looked up at Henry, his voice soft. "Do you think Mom can see us right now?"

Henry paused, his heart tightening. For a moment, he wasn't sure how to respond. The weight of Charlie's question hung in the air, fragile and delicate.

"I think she's with us, buddy," Henry said quietly. "I think she's always with us."

Charlie smiled, squeezing his father's hand. "I miss her."

"I miss her too," Henry whispered, his voice filled with emotion. He looked down at his son, realizing that in the midst of his own grief, he had neglected how much Charlie needed him—how much they needed each other.

The reindeer waited patiently on the shore as father and son stood in the center of the lake, surrounded by the magic of the night. In that moment, Henry felt something shift, a quiet understanding settling between them. This journey wasn't just about magic and wonder—it was about finding their way back to each other, about healing the wounds they had both carried for so long.

Henry knelt down, looking Charlie in the eyes. "I know I haven't been there for you like I should have. But I'm here now. And we're going to get through this, together."

Charlie's eyes filled with tears, but he smiled, nodding. "I know, Dad."

They embraced, the stars shimmering above them, the night filled with the quiet, comforting magic that Christmas brings—the magic of love, family, and hope.

AS HENRY AND CHARLIE stood in the center of the frozen lake, bathed in the quiet glow of the night, the air around them seemed to hold its breath. For the first time since the loss of his wife, Henry felt ready to open the door to the memories he had locked away so tightly. The ice beneath their feet was a canvas, and it was time to paint the picture of the past that Henry had kept hidden.

Henry knelt in front of Charlie, gently resting his hands on his son's small shoulders. His voice, when he spoke, was thick with emotion. "Charlie, there's something I've been holding back... about your mom. Something I should have told you a long time ago."

Charlie's eyes, wide and full of trust, locked onto his father's. He didn't say a word, but his silence asked everything.

Henry took a deep breath, staring out at the endless expanse of the frozen lake, memories flooding back. "Your mom... she loved Christmas. More than anyone I've ever known. Every year, she'd spend weeks decorating the house, wrapping gifts, baking cookies. She'd even drag me outside to look at the stars on Christmas Eve, saying that this night, above all others, held magic." He paused, his voice catching in his throat. "She'd stand just like this, holding my hand, and tell me to never lose sight of the wonder in the world. I think that's why I've struggled so much... after we lost her, I felt like I'd lost that wonder too."

Henry's gaze fell, his shoulders heavy with the weight of his grief. "I was so wrapped up in my own pain, Charlie. I didn't see that you were hurting too. I pushed you away when I should have pulled you close."

Charlie's lip quivered, and he finally found his voice, small and fragile. "I miss her, Dad. I miss her every day."

"I know, buddy. I miss her too," Henry whispered, his heart breaking as he watched tears fill Charlie's eyes. "But she wouldn't want us to be like this, would she? She'd want us to be happy... to celebrate Christmas the way she did. With joy, and love, and togetherness."

Charlie nodded slowly, his tears spilling over as he wiped them away with the sleeve of his coat. "Sometimes... sometimes I feel like if I talk about her, it'll make you sad. Like I'm reminding you she's gone."

Henry swallowed hard, his own tears threatening to spill over. "Talking about her doesn't make me sad, Charlie. It helps me remember how special she was... how much she loved us. And it's okay to feel sad sometimes. But we have to remember that she's always with us, in every little thing we do. When we bake her cookies, when we put up the tree, when we look at the stars on Christmas Eve... she's there."

Charlie took a deep breath, his hand slipping into his father's once more. "I'm glad we came here tonight, Dad. I didn't know it, but I think I needed this."

Henry smiled softly, squeezing Charlie's hand. "Me too. More than I realized."

They stood there, side by side, the icy surface of the lake reflecting the stars above. It was as if the universe had paused to hold this moment for them—a moment of understanding, of healing, of realizing how much they still needed each other.

Charlie looked up at the sky, his voice filled with a quiet wonder. "Do you think she's watching us right now?"

Henry glanced at the heavens, where the stars twinkled brighter than he had ever seen. "I think she's with us in every star, in every snowflake... and in every memory. She's always been with us, Charlie. And she always will be."

For the first time in what felt like forever, Henry felt a sense of peace wash over him. The pain was still there, but it wasn't as sharp—it had softened, woven into the fabric of his love for both his wife and his son.

The reindeer stood quietly at the shore, waiting patiently as the magical sleigh glimmered in the distance. Henry and Charlie knew it was time to head home, but something had shifted between them. They had walked through the pain together, and now, they were ready to move forward—carrying their memories with them, but no longer weighed down by the past.

"Ready to go home?" Henry asked, his voice lighter than it had been in years.

Charlie smiled, nodding. "Yeah, Dad. I'm ready."

Hand in hand, they made their way back to the sleigh, the stars twinkling above them as if giving their silent blessing. The reindeer pawed the ground gently, its bells jingling softly in the quiet night. As Henry and Charlie climbed back into the sleigh, the reindeer took off once more, lifting them into the sky with ease.

The frozen lake shimmered below as they soared through the night, the snowflakes falling softly around them like whispers of peace. Charlie leaned into his father's side, and Henry wrapped his arm around his son, holding him close.

For the first time in a long while, Henry felt the warmth of Christmas. Not just the lights or the decorations, but the true meaning of the holiday—the love that binds a family together, no matter what they've lost.

As the sleigh glided through the air, Henry looked down at Charlie, his heart full of gratitude. They had taken this magical journey together, and now, they were ready to face whatever came next, as father and son.

And above them, shining brighter than ever, the stars watched over their midnight sleigh ride, a silent reminder of the love that would always guide them home.

THE SLEIGH TOUCHED down gently in the snow-covered yard of Henry and Charlie's home, the same place where their magical journey had begun just hours ago. The house stood quietly before them, its windows glowing faintly in the early morning light. Dawn was approaching, and the first signs of Christmas Day shimmered on the horizon.

As the reindeer came to a stop, Henry and Charlie lingered in the sleigh for a moment, neither quite ready to leave the magic behind. But this time, the silence between them wasn't heavy or distant. It was full—of love, of understanding, of a bond that had been renewed.

Charlie looked up at the reindeer, its eyes bright and wise, as if it understood the gift it had given them. "Do you think we'll see him again next Christmas?" Charlie asked, a hint of wonder in his voice.

Henry smiled, glancing at the magnificent creature. "I think magic finds us when we need it most, Charlie. Maybe we will. Maybe we won't. But we'll always have tonight."

The reindeer dipped its head in a gentle farewell, its bells jingling softly as Henry and Charlie climbed out of the sleigh. As soon as their feet touched the ground, the sleigh rose again, carrying the reindeer into the sky. They watched as it disappeared into the clouds, the sound of its bells fading into the soft whispers of the wind.

Henry looked down at Charlie, who stood beside him, his face glowing with something Henry hadn't seen in a long time: hope. "Come on, buddy. Let's go inside," Henry said softly, and together, they walked toward their home.

Inside, the house was still and peaceful. The Christmas tree stood in the corner of the living room, its twinkling lights casting a warm glow across the room. For the first time since his wife had passed, Henry didn't feel the overwhelming weight of grief when he looked at it. Instead, he saw the joy and love that had once filled this house—and that would fill it again.

As they hung their coats and settled by the fire, Henry felt a lightness in his heart, a shift that had taken place during their magical sleigh ride. He glanced at Charlie, who was curled up on the couch, his eyes heavy with the exhaustion that follows a night of wonder. Henry moved to sit beside him, placing an arm around his son.

"Dad?" Charlie murmured, his voice sleepy.

"Yeah, Charlie?"

"I'm glad we did this. I'm glad we talked about Mom."

Henry's chest tightened, but not with sorrow—with gratitude. "Me too, Charlie. Me too."

Charlie yawned, resting his head on his father's shoulder. "I think this is going to be a good Christmas," he whispered.

Henry smiled, gazing into the soft glow of the fire. "It already is, buddy."

As Charlie drifted off to sleep, Henry stayed beside him, feeling the warmth of the moment. The house felt different now—not because anything had changed, but because everything had. The memories of his wife no longer haunted him; they comforted him. And for the first time, he realized that she wasn't truly gone. She lived on in the love between him and Charlie, in the traditions they would carry forward, and in every Christmas they would share from now on.

The first light of dawn crept through the window, and Henry knew that when Charlie woke up, they would open presents, bake cookies, and maybe even stand outside in the snow, gazing up at the stars the way his wife used to.

But for now, Henry simply sat, holding his son close, watching the fire crackle softly. The house was filled with peace, love, and the quiet joy that comes from remembering what truly matters.

As Christmas morning arrived, Henry realized that the magic of the night hadn't ended. It had just begun.

And for the first time in a long while, Henry felt ready to embrace the future, knowing that love—like the stars in the sky—never truly fades. It only grows brighter, guiding us home, wherever that may be.

And on this Christmas morning, Henry and Charlie were home—together, with hearts full of hope, love, and the magic of the season.

www.ingramcontent.com/pod-product-compliance
Lightning Source LLC
LaVergne TN
LVHW060040261225
828480LV00007B/89

9798227584359